SOFT SOAP FOR
A HARD CASE

Sam Heller had been hit — hampered in his speed of drawing and holding a gun. He and a homesteader faced Lance Russell and his trusty sidekick when they stepped out from behind a shed. Two against two, yet Sam didn't have a chance: he would always struggle to outdraw them. Meanwhile, Kate Bond waited, hoping for his return, whilst her beloved Sam was determined to go down fighting. Then Russell and his hired gunmen went for their guns . . .

*Books by Billy Hall
in the Linford Western Library:*

BILLY HALL

SOFT SOAP FOR A HARD CASE

Complete and Unabridged

LINFORD
Leicester

First published in Great Britain in 2011 by
Robert Hale Limited
London

First Linford Edition
published 2013
by arrangement with
Robert Hale Limited
London

British Library CIP Data

Hall, Billy.
    Soft soap for a hard case. - -
(Linford western library)
1. Western stories.
2. Large type books.
I. Title II. Series
823.9'2–dc23

ISBN 978–1–4448–1454–5

Published by
F. A. Thorpe (Publishing)
Anstey, Leicestershire

Set by Words & Graphics Ltd.
Anstey, Leicestershire
Printed and bound in Great Britain by
T. J. International Ltd., Padstow, Cornwall

This book is printed on acid-free paper

1

It was a good bet the horses were stolen. It was equally certain a cautious man wouldn't say so. They were obvious hardcases, all.

The four men sat their horses easily, ranged around the thirty or so head of horses, keeping them bunched. The obvious leader of the four, hands folded on his saddle horn with the reins between them, chatted amicably with the rancher.

'I don't recognize any o' them brands,' the sun-bronzed rancher offered. 'They ain't from around here.'

'Naw, they ain't,' the horse trader agreed. 'We been tradin' for a good piece a'ready. We started out north o' Laredo with seven good mules. We worked our way up through the Indian Nation, swung over into Colorado, along the east slope o' the mountains, there. We been on the trail for pertneart a year.'

'Uh huh,' the rancher fretted. It was obvious he was uncomfortable. 'What're you askin' for 'em?'

'If you can use the whole bunch, we'll let you have 'em for fifteen dollars a head. If you just wanta pick out some, they'll be twenty.'

'Uh huh. They all well broke?'

'Yup. Some better'n others, naturally. Some of 'em are good workin' horses. Some are rideable, but ain't been taught much. Them two roan geldings are right good ranch horses. They got a lot o' cow in 'em. The sorrel stud ain't so good for workin'. He tends to be pretty studdy, but he'd make a fine stud for buildin' a herd. Them three paint mares are gentle, but two of 'em are a mite lazy. Over all, it's a good bunch o' horses. We'll sell 'em for cash money or trade, if you got some you're wantin' to get rid of, or just want some new blood in your remuda.'

2

None of the four had failed to notice the half dozen ranch-hands that seemed to be drifting aimlessly around the ranch yard. As they appeared to be attending to various chores, they had positioned themselves so that they formed a large half circle. The horse traders and the small herd they were proffering were well covered, should a confrontation develop.

Watching his crew from the corners of his eyes, without appearing to, the rancher became more confident enough to broach what he considered the most important question at hand. He said it as a statement of fact, but it was an undisguised question. 'I 'spect you've got bills o' sale for all of 'em.'

The horse trader grinned as if there were no implied accusation in the question. 'Sure thing. And I'll sure give you a bill o' sale on any or all of 'em as well. They're sure clean.'

'They're clean, but they ain't yours.'

The words shot through every man in the ranch yard like a bolt of lightning.

All eyes swivelled as one to the speaker.

As if he were an apparition from out of nowhere, he stood facing the leader of the horse wranglers. Nobody present had ever seen him before. Nobody had seem him approach. That, in itself, seemed impossible, but there he stood.

His pale blue eyes were hard and flat. His posture was deceivingly casual. His left thumb was hooked in the front of a cartridge belt. It, in turn, held a well-worn Colt .45, tied low on his right thigh. His right hand hung relaxed just by its grip.

The leader of the horse wranglers moved his own hand nearer his gun butt. 'Whatd'ya mean, they ain't mine? I got a bill o' sale for every one of 'em. Who are you, anyway?'

'If you got a bill o' sale, you wrote it yourself,' the newcomer accused in a conversational tone, as if commenting on the weather or the price of beef. 'Them roan geldings and two o' the pinto mares belong to my boss. They

4

was stolen two weeks ago. I been trailin' you since.'

The horse trader glanced nervously around at the other three of his comrades, assuring himself they were well situated and ready for whatever action might be necessary. He turned back to the intruder. 'Are you callin' me a horse thief?'

The answer was as cryptic as it could possibly have been. 'Yup.'

The horse trader's hand gripped his pistol and started to pull it from the holster. It had scarcely moved enough for the cylinder to clear the top of the holster when he was knocked from the saddle by a slug from the newcomer's .45. Nobody had seen him draw it, any more than they had seen his arrival. It was just there, in his hand, a tendril of smoke drifting lazily from the end of the barrel.

That Colt had already swung to cover the nearest of the other three. Hands on their guns, the trio looked around in rising panic. Half a dozen guns were suddenly trained on them. Slowly, each released his grip on his pistol and raised his hands.

The rancher turned to the new-comer. 'Who're you? I didn't even see you ride up.'

Without taking his eyes from the surrendering wranglers, he said, 'I rode up behind the barn and walked from there. You was all pretty intent on watchin' one another. I been tailin' these boys since they drove off horses from the outfit I work for.'

The rancher digested the information a moment, then addressed the nearest of the dead man's companions. 'Where's them bills o' sale you boys got?'

The man swallowed hard, then said, 'They're in Red's saddle-bag I think. That's where he usually kept 'em.'

Without averting his eyes, the rancher called one of his hands. 'Clint, come take a look.'

One of the ranch-hands holstered his gun and walked to the dead man's horse. He lifted the flap on the left

6

saddlebag and rummaged briefly through its contents. His hand emerged with several pieces of wrinkled and dirty paper. 'Would this be them?' he asked.

'Bring 'em here and we'll see.'

The rancher looked over the writing on the several pieces of paper carefully. 'Now there's a real surprise,' his voice dripped with sarcasm. 'Every one o' these bills o' sale seem to be written by the same hand.'

He addressed the man he had spoken to before. 'Maybe you can tell me how six different bills o' sale, signed by six different names, can all look like they have the same man's writing.'

The man's face had paled in increments as the rancher spoke. From a visage almost devoid of color, he said, 'I don't know. Red, he took care of all that stuff.'

The rancher turned to the new-comer. 'What's your boss's brand?'

'Rafter J.'

The rancher nodded. 'I spotted that

brand on a couple at least.'

'I'd guess you'll find a Flying R, and a Rocking CJ too. They're two more outfits close to us that lost some horses about the time these boys rode through.'

One of the ranch-hands called out, 'I see two with the Rocking CJ.'

Another chimed in. 'There's a Flying R on a couple geldlings, and a Rafter J on the stud.'

The rancher turned back to the wrangler. 'You boys wanta come clean?'

The three looked at one another, then back at the rancher. Their choices were reduced to three, all equally devoid of any probability of survival. They could whip their horses around and run, hugging close to their animals' necks, hoping to escape pursuing bullets; they could try to shoot their way clear, or they could submit meekly to a noose.

They chose to go out fighting. All three grabbed their guns.

Instantly a roar of gunfire erupted

from the newcomer's weapon. It happened before any of the ranch-hands could squeeze a trigger. It ended before any of the horse thieves' weapons had cleared leather. It was all over before anyone but him had time to react. Three reports from the hunter's .45 blended together into one continuous sound. Three horse thieves slumped, then toppled from their saddles. Dust blossomed from beneath each of them as they sprawled on the ground at almost the same instant.

Every ranch-hand's head swivelled to stare at the newcomer. Jaws hung loose as if each had witnessed the impossible. The stranger casually ejected the spent brass from his .45, replaced each with a fresh cartridge, and dropped his pistol back into its holster. He addressed the rancher, still in that conversational tone, as if discussing the weather. 'I'll be cuttin' out my boss's horses, and the others I know belong to our neighbors, if you folks don't mind.'

After waiting a couple heartbeats, the

rancher said, 'You might take a look at the other brands, too. Spread the word on your way back that they're here, if their owners want to come an' claim 'em.'

The man's eyes were expressionless as he nodded. He turned and walked back to the side of the barn where his horse patiently waited his return. It, too, bore a Rafter J on its left shoulder.

2

Carefully, Sam looked over the house and yard. He could see it all well from his vantage point on the high knoll. The dozen head of horses busily took advantage of his allowing them to stop; they ripped off great mouthfuls of the tall grass, chewing and swallowing greedily.

The house looked well-built and solid, though small. Its log walls were well chinked. Its roof was straight, covered with thick shakes against whatever weather might prevail.

Twenty yards from the house, the corral fronted a modest barn. It was more of a cowshed, actually, than a bonafide barn. It offered some measure of shelter, but was open on the side that became part of the corral.

It was the outhouse behind the house that made him smile. The path to it was lined with some hardy variety of flowers, blooming bravely against the barren image of the rest of the yard. The same flowers ringed the outhouse, in three neat rows. 'I bet they don't help it smell none better,' he muttered past his smile. 'Especially in hot weather.'

After a moment he glanced again at the westering sun. It promised that fingers of darkness would enfold the land within the hour. He spoke aloud to his horse: 'Well, Dan, let's see if we can put up there for the night.'

He clucked to the small herd of horses, pushing them down the hill toward the open gate of the corral. They entered it reluctantly, clearly smelling the enticing cold water of the stream that ran fifty yards beyond.

Sam dismounted and set the bars in place across the gate of the corral. He turned to find himself faced with an extremely attractive woman, nearly his own age. He noticed the rifle cradled easily in the crook of her right arm before he was captivated by the rest of her features.

She stood half a foot shorter than he, but seemed to look him squarely in the eyes nonetheless. Her eyes were strikingly green, but her hair was nondescript, mousy brown. Unbidden, the thought leaped into Sam's mind, 'Eyes like that ought to have red hair.'

He whipped the hat from his head. 'Evenin', ma'am,' he greeted her. 'My name's Sam Heller. I got this bunch o' horses I took back from some horse thieves. They stole 'em from my boss down in the Indian Nation. I wondered if I might water 'em in the crick over yonder, then keep 'em in your corral overnight, so I can get some shuteye.'

The woman scanned the horses briefly, then brought her eyes back to his. As if without thought, she also shifted the rifle slightly, moving it to a more quickly ready position. Her question was both pointed and challenging. 'You work for three different ranches?' she asked.

Sam grinned. 'You read brands quick, ma'am. No, I work for the Rafter J. Hap Harvey owns the spread. The Flying R and the Rocking C J are neighbors of ours. They lost horses the same night we lost our best stud. I headed out trailin' 'em. I caught up with 'em a ways yonder, tryin' to sell 'em to the Mill Iron ranch.'

'What happened to them?'

'Them who?'

'The horse thieves.'

'They're dead.'

'Did you kill them?'

'Yes, ma'am. They didn't leave me no choice. The owner of the Mill Iron looked over their bills o' sale and saw they was all as phony as a three dollar bill. They figured out they was about to get hung, so they opted to go out with their guns a-blazin' instead.'

'And did they?'

'Well, no ma'am, they didn't. They wasn't quick enough to get any of 'em unlimbered afore they checked out.'

She studied his eyes for a long

14

moment more, then nodded. 'Go ahead and take them over to the crick and let them drink,' she said. 'They look like they could use it.'

Sam nodded. 'They've been pushed pretty hard. I'd like to let them fill up on that tall grass, too, before I corral 'em for the night, if you don't mind.'

'Go ahead,' she agreed.

'Thank you,' he offered, as he turned to remove the poles that constituted the corral's gate.

The horses responded instantly, filing out of the gate behind the big stud that led the way, heading directly for the alluring scent of fresh water.

As Sam mounted his own horse to follow, the woman said, 'When you get them corralled, come on over to the house. I'll have some supper ready.'

'Why, thank you,' Sam replied. 'That's mighty good of you. I could use a square meal.'

She nodded and turned back toward the house without replying.

Sam frowned after her as she walked

away, trying, but failing, to keep from watching the swing of her hips as she walked. 'I wonder where her husband is,' he muttered, then added, 'I wonder if she greets everyone with that rifle.'

Two hours later it was fully dark. The horses were watered and fed, though they would have gladly spent half the night gorging themselves on the lush grass. When the others were corralled, he watered his own horse, then picketed him where he could have ample access to the grass the rest could now only envy. Then he looked toward the house. The windows shone brightly yellow with lamplight, glowing against the darkness. Their glow wakened a longing for home in him that he hadn't felt for a long time. He stood a long moment, studying the picture, pondering the ache it aroused in him. Then he shook his head against the distraction and strode toward the front door.

There he paused, uncertain whether he should make some kind of noise and wait, knock, or just open the door and announce his presence. He couldn't ever remember being that uncertain about what to do before. The uncertainty made him uncomfortable, and made the knock he decided on more timorous than he intended.

Instantly the woman's voice responded, 'Come on in.'

He opened the door and stepped in, sweeping his hat off his head as he did so. 'I, uh, didn't see a wash-stand out there,' he apologized. It was apparent he had removed all the trail dust he could at the creek, nonetheless.

The woman motioned toward a pitcher and wash basin, with a clean towel laid out beside it. 'It's right over there,' she pointed.

As he laid his hat down and washed up, the aroma of the meal she had prepared made his stomach cramp and his mouth water with hunger. As he dried his face, he was surprised by a young boy's voice. 'Did you shoot them horse thieves, Mister?'

'Billy!' the woman remonstrated.

'Mind your manners.'

'I was just askin', Ma,' the boy defended. 'I was listenin' while you two was talkin'. He said they all got shot, but he didn't say who shot 'em. I was just wonderin'.'

'You don't ask questions like that,' his mother stressed.

'Why not? I just wanted to know.'

'Sometimes it's best not to ask too many questions,' Sam interjected. 'Some folks take it kinda personal when you do.'

Without giving the boy time to respond, he said, 'What's your name, son?'

'Billy.'

'Is that short for William?'

'Yeah, I guess it is.'

'But folks call you Billy anyway, huh?'

A sudden mischievous glint flashed in the boy's eyes. Trying to speak without grinning, he said, 'Sometimes, but that ain't what they always call me.'

'It isn't?'

'Nope. Ma, she mostly calls me 'Billy,

don't!' But Pa, he just mostly called me, 'Dammit Billy!' '

'Billy Bond, you know better than to talk that way!' his mother scolded as she cuffed the back of his head smartly.

Billy ducked away from her hand, giggling. Sam struggled mightily to keep from laughing.

'Please sit down,' she offered. 'Supper is ready.'

As they took their seats, she stared pointedly at the boy. Accordingly he folded his hands and bowed his head. Taking his cue, Sam bowed his head as well, as the woman said a brief grace. In the instant she said, 'Amen,' Billy said, 'Pass the biscuits, please!'

'Billy!' she remonstrated again. 'Company is always first.'

'How come? I'm hungry!'

Sam picked up the plate filled with steaming biscuits. 'I'll tell you what,' he suggested. 'You grab a couple, then I'll take some.'

'Thanks, Mister!' the boy said as he hurriedly grabbed a biscuit with each hand. One went immediately to his mouth; he bit off a large chunk of it as he put the other one on his plate.

'I'm sorry,' she apologized to Sam. 'Billy seems to think he can get away with anything since his father was . . . '

The sentence hung in the air, as if she were unable to speak the words.

Billy had no such reticence. 'My Pa got shot,' he announced between mouthfuls.

Sam shot a glance at the woman, holding his fork with a bite of food half way to his mouth. 'I'm plumb sorry, ma'am. How'd that happen?'

Tears instantly filled her eyes in spite of her best efforts. She shook her head. 'We don't really know,' she said. 'He didn't come home one evening, so we went looking for him. We found him about a mile and a half from the house. He had been shot. His own gun was out of the holster, but hadn't been fired.'

Sam frowned. 'Were you having trouble with anyone?'

The grief in her eyes was instantly

tempered by a flare of anger. Her lips tightened. 'There are two of the bigger ranches that have tried to buy our place, ever since we got the patent on it. It was probably one or the other of them, but we don't have any way to prove it. The marshal came and talked to us, but nothing else was ever done.'

'How long ago was that?'

'Not quite six months.'

'I'm sorry,' he offered again, even though the words sounded lame, even to himself. 'What are you and the boy going to do now?'

Her chin lifted. Her shoulders squared. She straightened in her chair. 'I'm not sure, but we'll be OK. I'm a long way from helpless. Between Billy and me, we can keep the cows taken care of for a while. The crick runs year-round, at least, it hasn't frozen clear over since we've been here. We have good winter range. The stock should be fine, with just occasional checking on them. By spring, with a decent calf crop, we'll be able to make a better decision about what to do.'

'Me and Ma can run this outfit just fine,' Billy asserted. 'I'm pertneart a man, and I can ride and rope and shoot a rifle plumb good. I done shot us a deer just last week, and me and Ma got it all dressed out and everything.'

His mother made a brave effort to smile. 'You do awfully well for your age,' she agreed.

Sam returned to his supper in awkward silence. Unsure of what to say, he opted to say nothing. It was glaringly obvious to him that a woman and a child could not possibly maintain even a small ranch alone, but he was equally sure she had no means with which to hire a hand. A moment of irrational anger welled up within him, that her husband would get himself killed and leave them in such a position. That emotion was followed by an equally irrational urge to find out who had shot him, and exact retribution.

He finished his meal hurriedly, and rose from the table. 'Well, ma'am, if you don't mind, I'll find me a spot over toward the crick to toss my bedroll, and see if I can get me a little shuteye.'

'You're welcome to,' she said. 'If you stop by the house in the morning, I'll fix you some breakfast before you leave.'

'Thank you. You're real kind.'

As he went out the door, Billy called out, 'G'night, Mister.'

'Good night, Billy Don't,' he responded.

He lay awake in his blankets for a long while, pondering their seemingly impossible situation. He woke twice during the night, still thinking about it.

3

Dawn streaked the eastern sky with shades of pink and orange as Sam rolled up his bedroll. At the edge of the creek he shaved and washed. He headed toward the house, then stopped in his tracks.

At the back of the house, a small wood pile was neatly stacked. It was pitifully small against the need that would become pressing in two or three months. There were no larger logs nearby that could be split to add to the meager supply.

Looking around, he could see plenty of dead-fall in the fingers of timber that approached the house, but he well knew the strength and effort needed to convert it into fuel for the stove that provided both cooking and heat for the small house.

He frowned, shook his head, and

started toward the house again. Half way there, he stopped, looked at the paltry wood pile again, and frowned anew.

The smell of frying bacon drew him to the house like a magnet. He tapped lightly on the door. Instantly the woman's voice bade him, 'Come on in, Sam.'

He stepped inside, removing his hat. She was lifting a pan of fresh biscuits from the oven. 'I just made some biscuits and gravy, and fried a little bacon. I hope that'll be breakfast enough for you.'

'That's way more than you had any need to do,' he protested. 'But it sure does smell good. You know, I don't even know your name. Except Mrs. Bond, that is. I'll be happy to just call you that, if you prefer.'

She smiled, and his heart inexplicably raced, as if it were somehow ignited by that expression. 'My name is Kate,' she said. 'I'm sorry. I forgot that I hadn't introduced myself.'

'Kate. The name suits you.'

'It does? Why would you say that?'

He shrugged. 'I don't know. It just seems to fit you.'

She giggled unexpectedly. 'Well, maybe that's because I've worn it long enough it's settled on to me pretty well.'

He struggled in vain to think of something to say that would spark that smile or that giggle again, but seemed suddenly tongue-tied. Finally he said, 'Billy still asleep?'

She nodded toward the loft. 'He'll wake up pretty quick. He usually does when he smells breakfast cooking. He always woke up as soon as I came down when he slept down here, but we've both slept in the loft since Ralph was . . . since he . . . left.'

Sam started to say, 'I'm sorry,' again, but bit his tongue. He'd already said that enough times. Instead, he said, 'It's gotta be hard on the boy.'

'It's hard on both of us,' she agreed at once, 'but we'll get by.'

'Uh, speaking of that, I couldn't help but notice your wood pile's pretty meager. Winter's gonna be down on you pretty soon, and you sure need a lot bigger pile of wood than that to get you through.'

Her eyes grew troubled at once. She sighed, as she set the biscuits and gravy on the table. 'I've been thinking about seeing if I could hire somebody from town to come out and cut some wood. Billy does OK with an axe for his age, but he isn't big enough or strong enough to cut as much as we'll need.'

With obvious discomfort, Sam said, 'Well, uh, Kate, ma'am, I was thinking some while I was getting washed up and shaved. I don't guess I got a tight schedule getting them horses back home. If it's OK with you, I'd be plumb willing to stay around a day or two and see if I can drag some of that dead-fall out of the timber and get a bunch of it chopped up for you.'

Her eyes grew instantly cautious.

'How much would you charge me to do that?'

He shook his head. 'Oh, I wouldn't take any money! I wasn't asking for a job. I'd be plumb happy to just do that for you and the boy.'

The caution in her eyes grew stronger, bordering between fear and anger. 'And just what would you be expecting in exchange for all that work?'

Her meaning struck him like a faceful of ice water. His face turned beet red. He stammered as he said, 'Oh, no, ma'am! I, uh, I wasn't thinking of anything like that there! I wouldn't never try to take advantage of someone like . . . I mean, I didn't even think of . . . I didn't mean . . . '

She broke into that radiant smile again. 'Oh, for heaven's sake sit down and stop stammering. I didn't mean to embarrass you. I just needed to know what you had in mind. I feel very defenseless, sometimes, being here with just me and Billy.'

Before he could answer, Billy bounded down the ladder from the loft. 'Hi, Mister,' he greeted Sam.

'Hi, Mister?' Kate challenged. 'Doesn't your mother even rate 'Good morning'?'

'Aw, I knowed you'd be here, Ma. I was just a-scared Sam'd already be gone when I woke up. You gotta leave this morning, Sam?'

Sam grinned. 'Well now, that's just what your Ma and I were talking about. I haven't had a good chance to chop wood and get my muscles loosened up for quite a while. If I was to stay a day or two and work on your wood pile, do you think you could keep my horses from wandering off? You know, keep 'em sort of bunched together, but not too tight, where they can fill up on grass and water?'

'Oh, boy! You bet! I can sure do that! Me'n Topper — that's my horse's name, Topper — me'n Topper can keep them horses o' yours wherever you want 'em. You gonna use my Pa's saw?'

'Do you have a tree saw?'

'Yup. One o' them two-man saws with the big tall handles on both ends. Me'n Pa'd cut logs up with it sometimes, but mostly it was him'n Ma. I get tired too quick, on account o' it's too high up for me when the logs are on them sawbucks. But me'n Topper can herd horses or cows or most anything like that all day long.'

True to his word, the boy and his horse kept the small remuda well in range throughout the day. Sam turned his own horse into the bunch, choosing instead another with the Rafter J brand, to let his mount rest. Using his lariat, he used that horse to drag three dozen fallen trees from the timber to the area behind the house. Then he picketed the horse and fell to work.

He hoisted the first of the trees on to the sawbucks, and began sawing it into stove-length sections. The saw was long and unwieldy, and he struggled to make it work well. He had just started the second cut when Kate came round the house. Without saying anything, she stepped to the other end of the saw and grasped the handle with both hands. The saw instantly became a completely different and efficient tool, slicing its way through the tree in a fraction of the time it had taken him to make the first cut.

Three hours later they had heaped up a substantial pile of stove-length logs ready to be split. Sam's shoulders and arms ached with the unaccustomed effort. He marveled at the strength of this woman, who kept pace perfectly with the rhythm of the saw and never seemed to tire.

'I gotta take a break,' he admitted finally, leaning back against the trunk of a tree the grew in the yard.

'I'll get us some water, then I'll have to go fix us some dinner,' she responded.

She carried the water bucket and dipper out and they took turns slaking their thirst. When they had done so, he said, 'Leave the bucket. I'll go fill it at the crick.'

'OK. I'll get dinner started.'

He was nearly back from the creek with the bucket of fresh water when he heard the horses approach. He set the bucket of water down beside a sawbuck. He put his shirt on and buckled on his gun, both of which he had shed while he worked. He carefully dried his hand, then checked the gun and dropped it back in its holster.

Kate had heard the approaching horses as well. She stepped out of the front door, her rifle cradled in the crook of her right arm, as they rode into the yard.

'Mornin', Mrs Bond,' the leader of three greeted.

The frigid chill in her voice was unmistakable. Her words were clipped and brittle as ice. 'Good morning, Mr Russell. What can I do for you?'

'Now that's not a very warm welcome for a neighbor,' he responded.

'You're not much of a neighbor,' she

retorted. 'What do you want?'

Anger tinged his features, but his voice remained smooth. 'Well, I wanted to offer you my condolences again on the loss of your husband.'

'Thank you,' she said, her voice and lips tight and unyielding.

'I also wanted to offer to help you out of a tight jam. I know you're in a pretty tight spot. To be totally honest, I'd sort of like to have this place. I'd be willing to pay you five hundred dollars cash for it. If I remember right, your buckboard disappeared the same time your husband went and got himself shot. If you sell out to me, I'll furnish you a buckboard and a team of horses, so you can load all your stuff, and you and the kid can clear outa the country.'

The level of Kate's anger visibly rose as the rancher spoke. 'Now just how did you happen to know that Ralph had the buckboard with him when he was shot? I don't remember telling anyone that. Does that mean you were there?'

Lance Russell looked startled and at

a loss for words for one brief moment. He recovered quickly. 'Now don't go tossin' accusations around, lady. I'm makin' a fair offer, and if you got any sense you'll take it, and you and the kid'll clear out.'

Kate shifted the gun, gripping its forestock with her left hand. 'You killed him, didn't you? You killed him so I'd have to let you have our place for a tenth of what it's worth.'

'I told you not to go makin' them kind of accusations, lady,' Russell countered. 'You ain't in any position to go gettin' all huffy. I ain't sayin' my boys here would love to have me give 'em the go-ahead to have some fun, you bein' all alone and all. I'm just sayin' you ain't really got no choice but to take my offer and clear out.'

Kate started to raise the barrel of her rifle, but was stopped by Sam's voice. He stepped out from behind the corner of the house. 'I believe the lady already said, 'No,'' he said. His voice was quiet, but taut with menace.

'Who the Sam Hill are you?' the startled rancher demanded.

'I don't guess that matters,' Sam said. 'What matters is that the lady said, 'No'. That means it's time for you and your flunkies to turn around and go crawl back under whatever rock you crawled out from under.'

As he talked, one of Russell's men sidled his horse slowly away from the other two, a move not lost on Sam. It came as no surprise when the gunman said, 'Do you want to see if you can put me under that rock?'

'I figured you were low enough you could walk under it standing straight up,' Sam replied.

The gunman responded to the taunt instantly but it was far too slow an instant. His gun had scarcely begun its lift from the holster when Sam's gun barked and the gunman was driven from the saddle to sprawl on the ground.

The other gunman and the rancher both grabbed for their guns, but stopped abruptly when they realized Sam's .45 had already swivelled to cover them. They both sat there, frozen, knowing they were dead if they tried to draw, and defeated if they didn't.

Sam's voice crackled with deadly threat. 'Lift them guns out real slow and let 'em drop on the ground, or I'll drop you both on the ground instead.'

After the briefest of hesitation, both complied. 'Now back your horses away from 'em.'

They reined their horses backward a couple lengths. 'Kate, get their guns.'

Kate lowered her rifle and walked forward picking up both pistols, she returned, being careful not to get between Sam and the others. 'Better get the other guy's too,' Sam instructed.

Wordlessly she walked around behind him and retrieved the dead gunman's weapon as well.

Sam addressed the disarmed duo. 'Now you boys pick up your rotten baggage and tie him across his horse, then get off this place and don't come back.'

Both men glared at him briefly, then moved to comply. As Sam watched them, his .45 continually trained on them, Kate moved ten yards to one side and trained her own rifle on them as well. She held it comfortably with the stock rested on her hip, her finger on the trigger, her left hand holding the fore-stock, visibly capable of firing from that position in an instant.

Nobody spoke until the pair had completed their grisly chore and ridden away, leading the dead man's horse with its macabre burden.

Just before they were out of earshot, they stopped. Russell turned in the saddle and shouted, 'Don't think you've heard the last of this. We'll be back.'

In answer, Kate threw her rifle to her shoulder and fired. Russell's hat flew from his head. Cursing loudly, he leaned forward. Beneath the urgency of suddenly applied spurs, the pair's mounts surged to a run, leading the dead man's mount in a cloud of dust.

After several moments, Sam said, 'You're either awful good with that rifle, or awful bad. Did you shoot the hat on purpose, or were you tryin' to kill 'im?'

Her anger dissolved in a broad smile that seemed more mischievous than anything. 'It sort of makes you wonder, doesn't it.'

He did, for a fact, wonder, as she turned and disappeared into the house to continue fixing their noon meal.

4

Sam wasn't sure what he should do. On the surface, it was clear he should return to the wood pile until dinner was ready, but his instincts cried out for him to follow Kate into the house. He chose to follow his instincts.

Kate walked inside. She stood her rifle against the wall beside the door, stepped away from it a short step and stopped. She folded her arms. She took a deep breath. Her shoulders began to tremble, slightly at first, then with growing tremors that rippled throughout her body. A deep sob caught in her throat as she fought to stifle it.

Acting purely on instinct, Sam walked around in front of her. He stepped up to her and placed a hand on each of her shoulders. 'You did good,' he said.

She looked up into his eyes. What she

saw there released the torrent of her emotions. She burst into tears and collapsed against his chest. Startled, he did the only thing he could think of doing. He wrapped his arms around her and hugged her to himself, holding her against the intensity of the emotions that wracked her body. Neither said anything. After a couple minutes, she wrapped her own arms around him, squeezing him to herself as if trying to pull his strength into the vast vacuum of helpless terror that yawned within her.

They stood that way for several minutes, as the trauma of the morning blended into the greater trauma of losing her husband, her fear for the future, her responsibility for a son, her need to be more than she could possibly be. It all poured out wordlessly in sobs and tears and shudders as he held her, willing his own strength to buoy her flagging, fractured spirit.

Slowly, then, she relaxed her grip around him. He responded by releasing her. She stepped back. She lifted her apron and mopped her face with it. 'I'm . . . I'm sorry,' she apologized. 'I don't usually fall apart like that.'

His response surprised her. 'One of the toughest and fiercest fighters I ever knew was like that.'

Her eyes darted upward and locked on his gaze. 'He was?'

'Yup. He could stand alone against a regiment o' the Mexican army, or a whole tribe of attackin' warriors without flinching, and fight like a demon, till the battle was over. Then, when it was all over, he'd slip off by himself someplace and just plumb fall apart. There ain't nothin' wrong with that.'

Her eyes dropped toward the cabin's floor. 'I hate being that weak.'

'That ain't weak,' he argued gently. 'You are one tough lady. But don't never be ashamed of bein' a woman too.'

She looked back up at him, then seemed suddenly embarrassed. 'I'll go ahead and fix us some dinner.'

Taking his cue, Sam said, 'I'll work on the wood pile till you holler.'

He split a fair pile of kindling before she called him for dinner. She rang the triangular dinner bell that hung in the yard. Within minutes Billy galloped into the yard. 'The horses ain't gonna go anywhere for a while,' Sam called to him. 'Your ma's got dinner ready.'

They ate a hearty and hasty noon meal, then returned to their tasks: Billy to watching the horses, Sam and Kate to the wood pile. By the time she quit to fix supper, they were both exhausted.

They had scarcely finished eating when they heard a horse approach. 'Now what?' Sam muttered, as he checked his gun.

Kate waited, preferring the light and Sam's presence to meeting whomever approached in the dark alone.

'Hello the house,' a voice called.

Softly, Kate told Sam, 'That sounds like Bobby Farmer.'

'Who's he?'

'One of Spalding's cowboys. He used

to come by to help Ralph once in a while. I've never been very comfortable around him, but he's never really bothered.'

'Hello the house,' the voice called again.

'Is that you, Bobby?'

'Yup. Sure is, Kate. Can I come in?'

'Sure, come on in,' she invited. 'We've got some supper if you're hungry.'

A young cowboy burst unsteadily through the door. He didn't see either Sam or Billy, as Sam had herded the boy and himself back into the shadows cast by the kerosene lamp. 'Aw, I ain't really hungry,' Bobby said, slurring his words ever so slightly. Sam clearly smelled the whiskey on his breath from across the room. Kate backed up a couple steps, startled by his obvious drunkenness.

'Not for supper, anyway,' Bobby went on. 'A little dessert sure would be nice, though. You gotta be gettin' pretty lonesome nights, what with Ralph gone and all.'

'I don't know what you mean,' Kate pretended.

'Aw, sure you do, Kate. You gotta know I ain't never been able to keep my eyes off o' you. I didn't never do nothin', what with you bein' married and all. But now that you're just as single as me, I figured I'd just ride over here and cure your loneliness and mine too, for a while.'

Kate drew herself up to her full five foot six. 'You can just figure differently, Bobby Farmer. You can just get on your horse and ride back where you belong.'

'Aw, now, don't go gettin' all standoffish. I know you've been wantin' me just as much as I been wantin' you. There ain't nothin' standin' in our way, now, Kate.'

As he spoke he strode forward and wrapped his arms around her, pinning her arms down and barring her from reaching her rifle. She struggled against him, but she couldn't move from the iron grip of his arms around her. The smell of whiskey on his breath was overwhelming as he fumbled for her mouth to kiss her.

A rough hand on his shoulder spun him around unexpectedly. As he spun, an iron-hard fist slammed into his jaw, sending him sprawling across the floor. Kate stepped back, gasping, wiping at her mouth with the back of her hand.

Bobby scrambled to his feet just in time to be knocked flat by a left hook from Sam's fist. He got to his feet more slowly. 'Who're you?' he demanded.

'I'm a friend of Kate's, that ain't about to let some two-bit drunken cowboy make a fool of himself with her. Now get out.'

'What business have you got bein' here?' the cowboy demanded.

'If it was any of your business, I'd tell you I'm just working for her for a few days. But since it isn't any business of yours, I'll tell you I'm Santa Claus. Now go get on your reindeer and beat it, or I'll beat you.'

He looked confused, trying to make sense of the strange words. Then he clearly considered making a fight of it, but thought better of the idea. He stumbled for the door. As he started through it, he turned back to Sam. 'Whoever you are, you better watch your back. You're buttin' in where you ain't wanted.'

He slammed the door. In a few minutes they heard his horse gallop away.

'Santa Claus?' Kate demanded. 'Santa Claus? You might at least have told him you were a hired bodyguard or something, so he'd think you'd still be here if he came back. And if you're Santa Claus, why is he riding a reindeer?'

'You will still be here, won't you, Sam?' Billy pleaded. 'You ain't gonna leave me and Ma here by ourselves, are you?'

Sam squirmed. 'I'll stay another day, Billy, and get a good pile of wood split up. But I've got those horses out there, and they don't belong to me. If I don't take them home, I won't be any better than the guys that stole them in the first place.'

'But me and Ma need you here,' Billy insisted.

'Your ma's one tough lady, Billy. She can take care of herself, and you too. I helped her out a little tonight, but if I hadn't been here, she'd have handled that cowboy. If she'd have needed help, I'm bettin' you would have hit him over the head with that iron skillet on the stove. You'll both be just fine.'

As he rolled into his blankets under the trees, along the creek, he felt like he was the biggest liar in Wyoming.

5

'Hello the house!'

Sam and Kate had heard the buckboard's approach. Sam had put his shirt and gun back on. Kate picked up her rifle and stepped around the corner of the house.

'Well, hello, Eva. Hello, Hi,' she greeted Hiram and Eva Spalding. 'What brings you two over here?'

Then, without waiting for an answer, she said, 'Get down and come in. I was just getting ready to quit cutting wood and get some dinner.'

'You're cutting wood?' Eva accused.

As if on cue, the sound of an axe splitting wood resumed from the back side of the house. Sam had watched and listened long enough to know Kate was talking to friends, then returned to the wood pile.

'Well, not by myself,' Kate confessed.

'I've had some help the past couple days. A man named Sam Heller is resting his horses, fattening them up a little on the tall grass over toward the crick, and cutting wood for his keep.'

Hiram frowned. 'Heller. He ain't by chance ridin' a horse with a Rafter J brand, is he?'

'Why, yes. Why?'

Hiram seemed suddenly uncomfortable. 'Uh, I was visitin' with Buck Hinsmeyer the other day. Some fella from somewhere down in the Indian Nation caught up with some horse thieves tryin' to sell a bunch o' stolen stock to the Mill Iron. Buck says the fella called 'em horse thieves, then shot all four afore a one of 'em could get off a shot. He said he's the fastest man with a gun he's ever seen or heard of.'

Kate nodded. 'Sam told me about that, when he asked to feed and water his horses.'

'He told you about that?'

'Well, I guess I asked him why he had horses with that many different brands.'

'You asked a question like that of a strange man you had not even met before?' Eva demanded, her voice filled with reproach, rose an octave and slipped unconsciously into her natural Mexican accent. 'Katie Bond, you could get killed asking questions like that of strangers! How did he not shoot you for asking that?'

Hiram recaptured the conversation. 'I ain't sure it's a good idea, bein' here alone with a hardcase like that, Kate. He ain't bothered you none, has he?'

Kate shook her head. 'He's been a perfect gentleman.' A hard edge gave her next words more stress than she intended. 'He did send someone else packing, though, that thought I'd be lonesome enough by now to be available.'

'Somebody tried to take advantage of you?' Eva demanded. 'Did he shoot him? Did you shoot him yourself, with your own gun?'

Kate laughed. 'No. He was drunk, or I'm sure he wouldn't have tried anything like that. Sam knocked him down a couple times and sent him packing.'

'Who was it, Kate?' Hiram demanded.

Kate hesitated a long moment. Obviously torn between refusing the demand and divulging information that could be severely damaging to a man in that country, she finally said, 'It was Bobby.'

Hiram's face suffused with anger. 'Bobby Farmer? Are you tellin' me one o' my own hands pulled a hair-brained stunt like that? Is that where he got that big shiner an' sore jaw he's sportin'?'

'He was drunk, Hi. I'm sure he wouldn't try anything like that sober.'

'Well, he won't be drunk on any wages o' mine, from here on,' Hiram vowed. 'I'll tie a can to his tail so quick he'll wonder how it happened.'

'That's not necessary, Hi.'

'It sure as he . . . uh, it is too necessary,' Hiram argued. 'No hand of mine can get away with somethin' like that. If he'd try somethin' like that with you, my own daughters ain't even safe with him on the place. I'm plumb sorry, Kate.'

'It's not your fault, Hi. Nothing came of it. Besides, Sam already took care of it.'

Bart Spalding, riding his horse beside his parents' buckboard, spoke for the first time. As soon as he opened his mouth, it was apparent that speech was a problem for him. 'I-I-I-I t-t-t-t-told you he wasn't n-n-no good, Pa.'

Hiram looked at the strapping, sandy-haired, six foot two inch frame of his youngest son. He bore no resemblance to Eva, nor to Eduardo, their eldest son, who favored his mother. Two boys from the same parents could not have been more opposite. Eduardo was small, dark, quick as a rattlesnake in his movements, self-assured and suave. Bartholomew, or Bart as he was known, was pale-skinned and freckle-faced, hulking as his father, and stuttered uncontrollably.

The same total lack of semblance in

appearance was true of their two daughters as well. They sat their horses beside Bart, listening, but not participating in the conversation. Katrina was somewhat large-boned, blond and blue-eyed like her father. She was attractive with a large, wholesome beauty that seemed as honest and open as the Wyoming sky. At sixteen she was as good a ranch-hand as any man, but her parents were beginning to screen the hands they hired more carefully.

Camilla was the spitting image of her mother. She looked every bit of her Mexican heritage, with rich olive skin, perfect features, and, at fourteen, a body that already turned men's heads wherever she went. Her greatest difference from Katrina was on the back of a horse. Camilla knew only two speeds a horse should travel: fast and faster. While Katrina was as easy on her horse as possible, Camilla demanded the utmost from hers, all the time. Hiram scolded her constantly for pushing her mount too hard. Except for that, she seemed to idolize her older sister.

From the time Camilla began to crawl, she had tried to imitate everything Katrina had done. It was only a matter of time until their father began calling Katrina 'Pete', and Camilla 'Repeat'. It had grown so until everyone now knew Katrina simply as 'Pete'.

When Hiram declined to respond to his younger son's assertions about Bobby, Eva spoke, bringing the conversation back to Sam. The Mexican accent in her voice became even more pronounced as she adopted a teasing tone.

'It sounds to me like this Sam happened by at a pretty good time, eh? Is he handsome?'

'Eva!' Hiram remonstrated.

Kate only grinned. 'Actually, he is.'

Then her face and voice grew more serious. 'He's every bit as incredible with a gun as Buck told you, too, Hi.'

'You've seen him use it?'

She nodded. 'Lance Russell and two of his hired gunmen just happened to stop in. It was the same day Bobby came over, as a matter of fact, earlier in the day.'

'Twice in the same day somethin' like that happens? What did that slimy snake, Russell, want?'

'My place. He offered to buy the patent on the land and all my cattle for five hundred dollars.'

Eva gasped aloud. 'Did you tell him what kind of worthless garbage he is?'

'I told him something like that. Then he threatened to let his hired gunmen take advantage of me to their hearts' content if I didn't take the offer. That's when Sam stepped around the corner and ordered them off the place. One of the gunmen decided to kill him, instead. He didn't even get his gun out of its holster before Sam shot him out of the saddle. I didn't even see him draw. It was just like his gun was in his hand by magic or something. He was way faster, even, than Eduardo. Where is he, by the way? Why isn't he with you?'

Hiram either didn't hear the question, or was too preoccupied with fretting over his own hand's attempt to take advantage of Kate, the same day Russell and his gun hands had shown up. 'You had to deal with that and one of my drunken hands in the same day?' he fussed.

Eva climbed down the wheel of the buckboard, walked over and put an arm around Kate's shoulders. 'I think you need to keep this Sam around, Kate. That is what I think. It sounds like he showed up at just the right time, just when you were going to need for him to be here. Who knows, maybe the angels sent him to you.'

Choosing not to answer that, Kate said instead, 'Why don't you and the girls help me get some dinner, Eva. Hi, you and Bart can go get acquainted with Sam. Tell me what you think of him.'

'You wantin' me to size him up for you, or you just gettin' rid of me so you four can do a bunch o' women talk?'

Eva chose to answer for Kate. 'You are being sent away so we women can talk without you foolish men telling us what we are supposed to think and to say,' she confirmed.

Muttering to himself, Hi motioned to Bart, who dismounted and tied his horse's reins to the wheel of the wagon. Together they strode around the house. Sam set the axe head on the ground as the pair rounded the corner of the house. Sweat coursed in rivulets down his tightly muscled torso. He pulled his neckerchief from where he had stuffed it in a rear pocket and mopped his face. He nodded to the newcomers. 'Howdy.'

'Mornin',' Hiram responded, stepping forward and thrusting out a hand. 'I'm Hi Spalding. H Bar V Ranch.'

Taking the hand and returning the strong grip, Sam said, 'Sam Heller. I work for the Rafter J, down in the Indian Nation.'

Bart shoved his huge ham of a hand forward as well. 'I-I-I-I'm B-B-Bart. H-H-Howdy.'

Sam took the hand, returning its iron-hard grip. 'Bart. That short for Bartholomew?'

'Y-Y-Y-Yeah, b-b-but it t-t-t-takes me ha-ha-ha-half a d-d-day to say all th-th-that.'

Not sure just how to respond, Sam said only, 'I'm glad to make your acquaintance, Bart.'

Speaking just slightly too fast, as if embarrassed by his son's stuttering, Hiram jumped in to reclaim the conversation. 'Indian Nation, huh? That's a long way from here.'

Sam nodded. 'I came up here trailin' some horse thieves that drove off some of our best horses, as well as a couple of the neighbors'. I got about half of 'em back.'

'I heard about that.'

'That's not surprising. Word gets around.'

Bart stepped forward and took the axe from Sam. Wordlessly he attacked the wood pile, splitting the cut sections of log with a speed and efficiency that made Sam's efforts seem like child's play.

The two men watched in silence for a moment, before Hiram spoke again. 'Yeah, word does get around in this country. Where are the horses now?'

'Billy's keepin' 'em from driftin' off too far, so I can get some wood cut.'

Hiram nodded appreciatively, eyeing the wood pile that was stacked higher than the house. 'That's a pretty impressive wood pile for two days' work.'

Sam nodded. 'Nothin' like what Bart would have piled up in that time, the way he swings that axe. But I have been pushin' it pretty hard. Kate ain't no slouch on a two-man saw, neither. She don't need to stop and rest near as often as I do. Anyway, her and Billy are gonna need a lot of wood to get through the winter. Seemed like the least I could do before I push on.'

Hiram eyed him appraisingly. 'You'll be headin' out before long?'

If Sam was offended by the probing

question, he gave no indication. 'Day after tomorrow, most likely. I Should have wood enough split and stacked by then. On the other hand, if she don't ring the dinner bell too quick, Bart may have it all done by dinner.'

'Kate tells me one of my hands made a jackass of himself a couple nights ago.'

'Bobby Farmer's one of your hands?'

'He was until today.'

'What happened today?'

'Nothin' yet. It's gonna, when I get home, though.'

Sam was thoughtful for a long moment. Finally he said, 'I'd like to tell you not to be too hard on him. He was some drunk. On the other hand, it was Kate he tried to force himself on, so I'd like to tell you to horse-whip 'im. I guess you gotta do what you gotta do.'

'I already know what I'm gonna do. I'll send him packin', and tell 'im if I ever run into 'im again, even workin' for another outfit in this country I'll shoot 'im down like a mangy coyote.'

Instead of responding, Sam walked

over to Bart. He held out his hand. 'I'll take a few swings, Bart. Let you catch your breath.'

'I-I-I-I ain't t-t-t-tired yet.'

'Yeah, I know, but you're makin' me look lazy.'

Bart handed over the axe with obvious reluctance. Sam grinned at him as he took the axe. 'Don't worry, I'll hand it back just as soon as I show you how this really oughta be done.'

The two took turns trying to outwork each other, trading jibes, and challenging Hiram to judge which was the best log splitter for well over an hour before the dinner bell rang an end to their good-hearted rivalry and newfound camaraderie.

6

'Sam, I'm worried.'

Sam stopped and set the head of the axe on the ground. He shook his head, sending a shower of sweat in all directions. He already had enough wood chopped to see Kate and Billy through the winter. Every day he told himself one more day and he'd gather his horses and leave the country. Every day he found himself less willing to do so. Deep down he knew the supply of wood for winter wasn't what was keeping him here.

Kate stepped forward. Using her apron, she reached up and wiped the sweat from his face.

'What's the matter?' Sam asked, surprised at all the feelings her closeness, the touch of her wiping the sweat from his face, aroused in him.

'Those are pretty heavy clouds

coming up,' Kate fretted, nodding off toward the south-west.

Sam turned and looked where she indicated. Towering thunder-heads lifted above the distant mountains. Stark white at the tops, they grew increasingly dark as they neared the ground, forming a solid black wall that blocked out everything behind it. At the upper edges of the thunder-heads, tatters of cloud feathered away and reformed constantly. Beneath those clouds, another layer scudded at right angles to the movement of the larger and higher ones.

'Pretty good storm comin', looks like,' he agreed.

'I'm afraid it's going to be really bad.'

'Lot o' wind in it,' Sam observed. 'Lot o' lightnin' too, most likely. Where's Billy? I told him he didn't need to watch the horses today.'

'He talked me into letting him ride up to the high meadows to check on cows.'

Sam frowned. 'That ain't a good place to be in a thunder storm.'

Kate nodded her head with obvious agitation. 'That's what has me worried. I don't know if he'll watch the clouds closely enough to know to head for home before it actually starts storming. By that time, it'll be too late to get away from it.'

Sam walked over and picked up his shirt. Pulling it on, he buttoned it as he said, 'I'll saddle up and find him. What end of the ridge will he most likely be at?'

Kate didn't answer for several heart-beats. She fought down the arousal that inexplicably rose up in her as she watched him button his shirt over his muscled, sweating torso. She shook her head as if to force the thoughts from her mind. 'I don't know,' she said. 'He'll be looking for wherever the cows are.'

Sam swung his gun belt around him and fastened it. He tied the bottom of the holster around his thigh, just above the knee as he watched her face. Half a dozen emotions surged in him as well, as he studied the expressions that took turns crossing her beautiful face. He remembered the feel of her body against his when he had held her, after he had rescued her from Russell and his gun hands. He wanted with everything in him to offer her the haven of his arms now, but knew time was of the essence. He wasn't at all sure what her reaction would be in any case.

His voice was more gruff than he intended when he spoke. 'I'll find him.'

He walked with long, hurried strides to retrieve his horse. In ten minutes he was in the saddle, loping through the long grass toward the high meadows.

As he rode, he continually glanced over his shoulder at the approaching clouds. He measured in his mind the speed with which the storm approached and the distance he had to cover. After the first half mile, he nudged his horse with his spurs, urging him to an all-out run instead of the easy canter he had started with.

Half an hour later gusts of cold wind swirled intermittently around him.

Light dimmed as the dense clouds blanketed out the late summer sun. Lightning flashed in an almost constant display to his south-west; thunder rolled and rumbled.

Seeing a particularly bright flash of lightning, Sam counted in his head, measuring the time from the flash of lightning to the sound of its thunder.

Almost as if sensing his rider's fear, the big gelding he rode perceptibly increased the speed at which he was running.

'Hate to run you this way, fella,' Sam muttered. 'Especially uphill, but we gotta get to that boy. Kate ain't gonna be able to take it, if anything happens to him.'

Not long after that the first huge drops of rain began spattering against the dry ground. In some part of his mind it amused Sam that drops of water would cause small dust clouds to explode from the ground when they struck.

The rest of his mind was wrapped in

a thick mantle of fear. Lightning flashed in the air all around him. Once, a brilliant bolt of lightning struck a boulder standing high on a hill top. It formed a ball of fire that jumped to another boulder, then another, then another, in a series of explosions that threatened to deafen him. The thunder that followed instantly behind it did its best to finish the job on his hearing.

Watching the ridges ahead of him, he finally spotted Billy. Following a hog-back that led from the high ridge, he appeared to be trying to find a way to lower ground. Instead of bettering his position though, he was exposing himself as the highest thing around, almost guaranteeing that he would be the first thing to attract lightning.

Sam yelled his name against the wind that was now driving rain in sheets, but his voice was lost in the fury of the storm. The rain quickly obscured the boy, so he couldn't even see him.

He reined his horse in a direction intended to intersect the path the boy was following. Muttered prayers escaped his lips without his even being aware. They were interspersed with curses at the boy's callow inexperience, at his mother's allowing him to be out here alone, at his own slowness in finding him.

He rode through the bottom of a gully, already starting to run with water, and urged his horse up the other slope. Almost at the top he nearly collided with the mare Billy was riding. Each saw the other at almost the same instant.

The stark fear stamped on Billy's face gave way instantly to one of intense relief. That relief was felt just as strongly in Sam, but his face remained impassively stern. 'Get down off this ridge!' he yelled above the fury of the storm.

'What?'

'Get down!'

'Off my horse?'

'No! Get to lower ground.'

'Where?'

'Follow me.'

He turned his horse and headed back down into the gully. A fair sized stream, brown with mud, now flowed swiftly along the bottom. He turned his horse along it, following it downhill. He kept glancing over his shoulder, making sure the boy was following.

Visibility reduced to a few feet on any side, as the rain dumped prodigious quantities of water, interspersed with occasional hailstones. Lightning flashed in a continual pyrotechnic display that made eyes and heads ache; thunder shook the ground.

Almost running into the first of the trees, Sam encountered a stand of timber, just where the gully they were following widened out into a broad swale. Entering the cover of the trees, they found their first respite from the storm's fury.

Without pausing, Sam pushed into the timber, following it to his right where the ground rose toward another ridge. Half way up the side of the hill, beneath a dense stand of pines, he swung from the saddle.

Riding up beside him, Billy lunged from his own saddle into Sam's arms. He was shaking so hard Sam thought for a moment he might be having some kind of fit for a moment. When he saw that wasn't the case, he wondered whether it was fear or cold from the icy rain that prompted the violent trembling.

Not knowing what else to do, he simply wrapped his slicker around the boy, willing his strength and courage to reassure the lad. In moments, Billy's trembling subsided. Embarrassed, he pushed away from Sam's grip and stepped back.

'Wow!' he exclaimed. 'That's some storm!'

'It ain't over yet,' Sam reminded him. 'Let's take cover under that pine tree. It'll keep some o' the rain off of us.'

Billy hesitated. 'I thought we wasn't s'posed to take cover under a tree in a lightnin' storm.'

Sam nodded approvingly. 'That's

exactly right, if it's a tree standin' out alone. That makes it the highest thing around, and that's what lightnin' always strikes. But when there's a bunch o' timber like this, it's the higher trees that are most likely to get hit. Usually the ones close to the top, close to rocky outcropping or somethin' like that.'

'Oh,' Billy responded, moving under the tree where Sam had already settled on to the ground, his back against the tree.

Billy sat down almost against him, leaning against the tree so their shoulders touched. 'I'm glad you found me,' he confessed, as if acknowledging some grave weakness.

'Me too,' Sam agreed. 'I pertneart lost it when your ma said you was up here in the high country, with that storm a-comin'. By the way, you ridin' along that ridge thataway was just beggin' lightnin' to strike you. When you first see clouds like that formin', you best be beatin' it to lower ground somewhere.'

'I wasn't payin' attention till the thunder got loud,' Billy admitted. 'Sorry.'

'Don't worry about it. We got you down off o' there in time.'

There was silence between them for several minutes. Tentatively, then, Billy said, 'Did you ever know anyone that actually got struck by lightning?'

Sam glanced sideways at the boy, as if measuring him. Finally he said, 'Yeah, I've known half a dozen men that did. Most of 'em couldn't get to lower ground, or were out on the flats, tryin' to keep a herd from stampedin' in the storm.'

'That's awful! To get killed, just doin' your job, I mean. It don't seem fair.'

'Life ain't never fair, Billy.'

After another long pause, Billy said, 'Did you ever know a kid that got struck?'

Sam shot him an oblique glance. He took a deep breath. His voice low and fraught with emotion, he said simply, 'Two.'

'Two kids?'

'Yup. Brothers.'

'What happened?'

'Their pa sent one of 'em out after the milk cows, 'cause there was a storm comin'. When he didn't get back when he thought he should have, he sent his brother after him. Lightnin' hit 'em when they was almost home with the cows. Killed both boys, both o' their horses, and one o' the cows.'

'Wow! That's awful! Did you know them?'

'Yup. They was neighbors to us.'

In a typical child's way of fussing over irrelevant details, Billy asked, 'Did they have both funerals together?'

Sam didn't even smile at the irrelevance of the question. 'Yeah, they did. That was the only funeral I was ever at where someone didn't take off his hat.'

'Who didn't take off his hat?'

'Their pa. He just sat there, staring, the whole way through the funeral. I don't think he even knew he'd left his hat on. Someone had to tell him when the funeral was over. Someone took his arm and got him to stand up and walk out.'

'I bet he felt like I did when my pa got kilt.'

'Yeah, I 'spect he did. But you're a stronger man than he was.'

'What do you mean?'

'I mean you toughed it through. He couldn't.'

'He couldn't? Why? What'd he do?'

It was again a long moment before Sam said, 'The next morning his wife realized he hadn't come to bed. She went out looking for him. She found him in the barn. He'd shot himself.'

'He shot himself? Why?'

'He blamed himself for getting his boys killed. He sent them after the cows, and he just couldn't live with thinking he was responsible for their deaths.'

'But it wasn't his fault! He didn't know they'd get struck by lightnin'.'

'I know that. He just wasn't able to

think it through that well.'

Again there was a heavy silence. With, again, his boyish simplicity, Billy said, 'I wish I'da been there. I coulda told him that it'd start hurtin' less after a while. It don't stop hurtin', but it hurts some less after a while.'

Then more faintly, his voice fading as he said it, 'I wish I coulda told 'im that.'

Fighting down his own emotions, Sam heaved himself to his feet. 'I think the worst of the storm's past. We'd best be headin' back to the house. Your ma's gotta be worried sick about you.'

'About both of us,' Billy corrected.

It was obvious to Sam that he was the one who was right. When they first came into sight of the house, Kate burst out of the door on a run. She ran to meet them, catching Billy as he lunged from the saddle into her arms. She stood there, holding her son, sobbing out the fear she had not allowed herself to surrender to until then. When Sam had gotten their horses unsaddled, they were just walking into the house, her arm still around his shoulders, he could not have explained the overwhelming rush of loneliness that swept over him at being excluded from that small celebration.

7

'I need to check the cattle in the high meadows.'

Sam set the axe head on the ground and turned his attention to Kate. He tried unsuccessfully to swallow the lump in his throat that seemed always there when he looked at her. He couldn't explain her effect on him. He was helpless to keep his eyes from scanning up and down the length of her body, then settling on the magical depths of her eyes, every time she approached him.

He forced his mind to what she had said, instead of the myriad images that clamored for primacy in his thoughts.

'I could use a break.' He tried to sound casual. 'Mind if I ride along?'

The change in her expression betrayed her hope that he would offer exactly that. 'I'd like that,' she responded. 'Maybe

Billy would like to ride along too. I think he's getting a little bored just watching your horses.'

Sam nodded. 'He was all excited about it the first day. By now he's figured out they aren't going anywhere as long as they've got all that good grass and water.'

She nodded in agreement. 'I'll pack us some lunch. There's a spring up there with really good water. We can call it a picnic, as well as checking on the cows.'

'Don't know how a man could resist an offer like that,' he grinned, fighting down the sudden and surprising resentment that Billy would be coming along.

Half an hour later they trotted from the yard together. Along the way she kept up a lively commentary on the features of her range. She pointed out where they brought the herd for calving, she indicated the most sheltered areas for winter range. Billy showed him where he had shot his first coyote, just as it was attempting to sneak up on a newborn calf without being seen by the calf's mother.

'Mountain lions and coyotes got almost half of our first year's calves,' Kate told him. 'It took us the first two years to get their numbers cut down enough we could afford the losses.'

'There's gettin' to be enough ranches in the country they ought to be gettin' 'em thinned out,' he observed.

'They're not as bad as they were,' she agreed, 'but they still get plenty. It really makes me mad when they kill baby calves that aren't old enough to try to run.'

'Easy prey,' he muttered, with the westerner's universal hatred of the predators.

They reached the spring without seeing any cattle. He could tell by the way she kept scanning the horizons that she was getting concerned. She tried to keep it from showing as she pointed out the promised location of their spontaneous picnic.

Reddish rocks thrust upward out of

light brown clay, forming a rugged ridge that reached thirty feet upward. In a semicircle of the monolithic upthrusts, ice cold water flowed, forming a crystal-clear pool thirty feet in diameter. The lower end of the pool flowed into a rivulet of water that meandered along for three quarters of a mile before being absorbed into the eternally thirsty soil. For that three quarters of a mile brush and grass proliferated, making a slash of brilliant green in the middle of a more arid table land.

Tracks of cattle, as well as those of deer, antelope, elk, bear, cougar, coyote, and other animals attested to the popularity of the ever-present water. Numerous bones in varying stages of sun-bleached whiteness bore witness to predators' awareness of the consistent drawing power of that water, attracting the prey they sought.

'I never have figured that out,' Sam pondered aloud.

'Figured what out?' Kate responded.

Sam watched the spring water surging up out of the ground for a long moment. He turned, looking at the surrounding country. 'Well, water runs downhill, right?'

'Well, yes,' she replied, as if stating something far too obvious to need stating.

'So here we are, high enough to see the country for miles around. This is probably the highest point this side of the mountains yonder. And up here on this high point, water comes bubblin' up outa the ground. Where's it comin' from? How does it get up here?'

Kate frowned at the spring as if it had somehow offended her. She looked back at Sam. 'I never really thought about it. I always figured the springs in the mountains came from snow melt higher up, but there isn't any 'higher up' here. I don't know.'

'And it's ice cold,' Sam stated, as if adding to an imponderable mystery.

'Springs is always plumb cold,' Billy announced with the absolute certainty of an eight-year-old.

Kate smiled, but shook her head. 'I've heard there are springs up north where the water comes out of the ground boiling hot.'

Sam nodded. 'I've heard of them. There's a spot I heard about over in Dakota Territory that's even stranger.'

'What's that?'

'Well, from what I've heard, there's a spot at the south end of the Black Hills, where hot springs come up outa the ground. They've built some bath houses there, and such, where people go. It's supposed to be good for what ails 'em. The crick is called 'Hot Brook'. Then there's another canyon that runs parallel to it, less than a half mile away. There's a bunch of springs in it too, but they're ice cold. That crick is called 'Cold Brook'. So you've got Hot Brook and Cold Brook comin' up outa the ground within half a mile of each other, and both runnin' to the Cheyenne River. The fella that was tellin' me about it swore up an' down it's the Gospel truth.'

'That's plumb funny,' Billy interjected.

'That is really strange,' Kate agreed.

'Almost as strange as sittin' here talkin' about hot and cold water instead of eatin' that lunch you brought,' he brought her back to the present.

Kate giggled. 'Just like a man. Always thinking of your stomach.'

Sam started to retort, 'Not always,' but decided against it. Instead he just grinned in response. For the next half hour they ate, talked, and thoroughly enjoyed each other's company. It was not lost on Kate that Billy chose to sit almost against Sam, instead of next to her.

By the end of the half hour she began to grow antsy. 'I really am concerned about why we haven't seen any cattle,' she fretted.

'Does seem odd,' he agreed. 'Cattle tracks at the water are several days old.'

The return of that concern goaded them into action and ten minutes later saw them again in the saddle. They had ridden less than a mile when Sam veered off to one side. He rode a hundred yards that direction, then guided his horse in a large circle.

'What are you looking at?' Kate called.

He rode back next to her, Billy trailing immediately behind him, before he answered. 'I think we got a problem.'

'What?'

'Rustlers.'

Her sharp intake of breath betrayed the impact of the word. 'Why?'

'Somebody's been hazin' cattle that-away. Let's see where the tracks go.'

She was a woman of the west, but she was not a tracker. Unable to see what tracks he meant, she was content to let him lead the way. Within another mile even she could clearly see the trail left by a large bunch of cattle being driven. 'They must have rounded up fifty or sixty head,' she offered.

'At least that,' Sam agreed. 'They've stopped gatherin' and they're movin' 'em outa the country.'

'How long ago?'

'Not long at all. Today, I'd say.'

'Can we catch up to them?'

'Easy. They can't move that many cows nearly as fast as we can ride. Don't get in a hurry, though. We don't know who they are or how many. We don't want to ride up on 'em too fast.'

She was content to let Sam take the lead. 'Billy, I want you to stay behind me.'

'But, Ma! I wanta ride up there with Sam.'

'You heard me.'

Reluctantly Billy dropped back to half a length behind her. His expression eloquently announced his discontent with the arrangement, however.

Two hours later they began to hear distant sounds of cattle being driven. Kate pulled her rifle from its scabbard. She checked the chamber to assure herself it was loaded, then let it rest across her legs, between her and the pommel of the saddle.

Billy started to do the same with the twenty-two caliber rifle he carried, but she stopped him. 'Billy, you leave that gun where it is. You're not going to get involved in anything with guns. And if I tell you to get down, I want you to get off your horse and lay down on the ground. Is that understood?'

'But Ma! I can shoot good.'

'You heard me.'

Billy silently and mockingly mouthed, 'You heard me,' in silence. His face was red with anger, but he held his silence.

Glancing at the sky, Sam estimated little more than an hour of daylight left. He dropped back beside Kate. 'Is there any water ahead, where they might settle 'em in for the night?'

She nodded. 'There's a basin another mile ahead, with a really big old buffalo wallow in the bottom. It's usually full of water unless it's been an awfully dry year. We've had a lot of rain this summer, so it'd be a good spot.'

Accordingly he was content to match the pace of the herd, keeping at least one hill between it and them. When the sounds and the decreasing dust being raised indicated they were, in fact, bunching them for the night, he dismounted. 'You two hang tight for a little bit. I'm gonna slip up on that ridge and see what I can see.'

They watched as Sam worked his way up the slope, removing his hat at the top so he could peer through the low sage without being seen. He stayed motionless there, watching, until the lower slopes were bathed in deep shadows. Then he worked his way backward until he could stand and walk without being seen.

'How many are there?' Kate asked.

'Five of 'em.'

'Are they camping in the cotton-woods?'

He nodded, noting with approval her knowledge of the land she ranched. 'Right at the north end of 'em.'

'There's a draw that runs almost to the trees there. We could walk up that draw and be almost in their camp before they had any chance of seeing us.'

'You're readin' my mind,' he nodded, 'except for that 'we' part. This isn't something for a woman. They've set one man out to watch the herd. Once it gets good and dark, I'll take him outa the mix first.'

Her eyes flashed. 'Those are my cattle, Sam Heller. Billy will stay with the horses, and the two of us will deal with the rustlers. And don't try to argue. The only way you can keep me from going with you is to tie me down, and if you think you can get that done you've got another think coming.'

He studied the set of her jaw and the flash of her eyes for a long moment, thinking of a lot of things other than rustlers and cows. He decided not to offer any answer, certain he could keep her with Billy and out of danger when the time came.

A whiff of wood smoke drifted on the breeze. Kate lifted her head. 'They're fixing their supper. They'll all be in their blankets within an hour.'

He nodded. 'We'd just as well loosen the cinches and let our horses rest and graze. I'll go take care of the night hawk when it's good and dark.'

They sat down on the ground together, talking softly, acting as if they had not a care in the world until it was fully dark. 'Guess it's about time,' Sam said, standing. 'Moon'll be up in another hour. Be better to move while it's still good and dark.'

He moved off into the night as silently as a shadow. He crawled over the top of the ridge, careful not to silhouette himself against the night sky, just in case the rustler with the herd might be looking his way. While he had been on the ridge earlier, he had mapped out a route in his mind for approaching the most likely position of the night hawk. Once below the top of the ridge, he moved with speed and confidence that was surprising over ground he had never covered before.

It took him a scant fifteen minutes to

reach the spot he wanted. Squatting in the edge of a tall clump of sage, he watched and listened intently. Almost immediately he heard the squeak of saddle leather, approaching from his right. He watched that direction, remaining motionless.

In the near total darkness, the night hawk was less than a dozen feet from him when Sam was able to pick out his form. He waited until the rider had passed almost by him, then stepped forward abruptly. He reached up and grabbed the man's belt before the rustler had any inkling of his presence. Even his horse had not sensed Sam's approach. As he did so now, the mount snorted and shied violently away from Sam's unexpected presence.

The sudden hold on his belt coupled with the horse's leap sideways unseated the rustler before he even had a chance to grab for the saddle horn. He hit the ground with a heavy thud. He immediately tried to surge to his feet, but Sam's gun barrel connecting smartly with the side of his head ended all such effort. He crumpled silently into a motionless heap.

Sam strode to the nervous mount, crooning softly to allay his fears. He removed the man's lariat from the saddle, quickly tied him hand and foot, then strode away.

He knew Kate and Billy were waiting for his return but instead of returning to them, he headed straight for the draw he had already spotted before Kate suggested it. By the time they realized he wasn't coming back for her, he should have the rustlers fully dealt with.

He eased into the bottom of the draw as silently as possible. Even then, he was painfully aware of the small avalanche of dirt his movements released. He waited motionlessly until it stopped and silence returned. He started to move on when a voice to his right nearly caused his heart to stop.

'I'm right over here,' the very soft voice informed him.

He recognized Kate's voice instantly. Then he nearly collapsed with a surging mix of emotions he made no effort to separate or analyze. He started to bark at her, half a dozen angry admonitions fighting each other for release. Even as he did, he knew any conversation reduced their chances of surprise. He also knew there was no way to send her back. He was left with no choice but to accept her presence with him. He refused to admit to himself he was actually glad for that presence.

Silently he moved along the bottom of the draw. When he had reached what he guessed was the closest point to the probable campsite of the rustlers, he looked at her in the darkness. He felt, rather than saw, her nod agreement.

Making as little noise as possible, they worked their way, side by side, up the side of the draw. At the top they peered cautiously over the rim.

Less than fifty feet away the embers of the dying campfire glowed softly. In the near total darkness, those embers gave surprising ability to make out the forms of four sleeping men. Sam studied the scene carefully for three or four minutes before a plan formulated itself in his mind.

Wordlessly he moved over the rim of the draw and crept forward. Kate stayed close behind him, letting him take the lead.

At the edge of the camp, Sam motioned for her to stop. He crept forward, into the center of the camp itself. He had noted that all four men were on one side of the fire. Working from the other side of it, he silently and carefully placed several pieces of wood on to the glowing embers. By the time he had worked his way back to Kate, the embers had ignited the new source of fuel. The fire came to life, casting a flickering glow over the sleeping men. The effect was to cast them in light, while he and Kate were outside its reach, standing in darkness.

He breathed into her ear, 'Watch the men. Don't look at the fire.'

She nodded, understanding the wisdom of not letting her eyes accustom to light.

When the fire had brightened the area, one of the rustlers abruptly raised up on one elbow. He looked around quickly, obviously confused that the fire was burning brightly again.

Sam waited no longer. He fired his .45 into the fire, scattering sparks and embers in all directions. At the same time he yelled, 'On your feet, you four. You're surrounded. Throw up your hands.'

All four boiled out of their blankets, guns in hand, eyes darting in all directions.

'Drop the guns!' Sam ordered.

Two men did so. Two fired instead, at the sound of Sam's voice. Sam's .45 and Kate's rifle barked at almost the same instant. Two men folded up and dropped to the ground.

The other two threw their hands as high as they could reach. 'Don't shoot!' one of them called out.

'Step over toward the fire,' Sam ordered.

The two did as told. As they neared the fire, they exchanged a quick glance. Moving as one, they dove behind the fire, using it to momentarily conceal themselves. The instant they hit the ground they rolled to their feet and began running, directly away from the fire, trying to keep it between them and the threat that had appeared out of nowhere.

Kate jerked the rifle to her shoulder, but Sam laid a hand on her arm. She looked at him sharply enough that the darkness couldn't conceal her question.

'Let 'em go,' Sam said. 'I got no stomach to hang 'em tonight, and they'd be a passle o' trouble gettin' to town. They're stockin' footed and unarmed. If they can get back to whoever sent 'em after your cattle, they just might mend their ways.'

Kate looked at him in unabashed amazement. 'Sam Heller, you are supposed to be a hardcase. I'm supposed to be the timid and tender one.'

'The good-smellin' soft-soap one,

anyway. Even now you smell plumb good.'

'Don't change the subject! You're just going to let them get away?'

'I 'spect we already did. Let's gather up their guns and get back to Billy.'

'What about the one watching the cows? Did you kill him?'

'Nope. I wrapped my gun barrel around his head, pulled his boots off and tossed 'em in the brush, and left him hog-tied.'

'Then we'll have to go get him. We can't leave him there to die.'

'Now who's goin' soft?'

'Well, we can't!'

'I wouldn't, anyway. I'd guess the two that took off runnin' will find him and take him along. If not, we'll haul 'im to town and turn 'im over to the marshal, along with these two.' He nodded toward the bodies of the two dead rustlers.

'Then we have to drive my cattle back home.'

'Gonna be a long night,' he observed, moving toward the rustlers' horses.

8

'You'd think this place was on a main road,' Sam grumbled. He reached for his gunbelt. He stepped where he could see the approaching rider as he secured the weapon around his waist.

'This one's wearin' a badge at least,' he muttered.

Kate stepped out of the door of the house, her rifle cradled in the crook of her elbow. 'I wonder if she gets tired o' havin' to greet everyone that comes along that way,' Sam pondered silently.

Aloud, he said, 'Looks like a lawman.'

'How can you tell?'

'Caught a flash of sun off his badge.'

She took a step backward and stood the rifle inside the door of the house. They stood side by side watching the approaching rider. He appeared relaxed in the saddle, but as he drew closer

Sam noticed the lawman's restless eyes constantly scanned everything around and ahead of him.

He reined in with a nod of his head. 'Mornin', folks.'

'Good morning, Marshal,' Kate responded, reading the legend 'United States Marshal' emblazoned on the gold badge. 'Get down and come in. The coffee pot's still warm.'

'Can't turn down an offer like that,' the marshal responded.

His extraordinarily large handlebar mustache that extended clear to the bottom of his jaws bore well stained testimony to his love of either coffee or chewing tobacco.

Kate stepped into the house, and he followed, sweeping the broad-brimmed, high-crowned hat from his head as he walked through the door. Sam followed, sending one last glance around to assure himself the marshal was alone.

'Nice place you folks have here,' the marshal observed, seating himself in the chair Kate indicated. 'I'm Harm

Denton, by the way.'

'I'm Sam Heller,' Sam offered, extending his hand to return the marshal's solid grip. 'This is Kate Bond. Actually, it's Kate's place,' Sam explained. 'I'm just sorta helpin' out for a few days.'

The marshal eyed him appraisingly, his expression betraying nothing of his thoughts. 'That so? You a drifter?'

'Not really. I work for the Rafter J down in the Indian Nation.'

The marshal's eyebrows rose. 'That's a purty good distance from Wyoming. Who's your boss?'

'Hap Harvey owns the place. Thad Messmer's the straw boss.'

'That name rings a vague bell,' the marshal mused. He picked up the steaming cup of coffee Kate had set before him, blew across the top of it and slurped off a sip of the dark, slightly cooled liquid. 'How many cows you run down there?'

'Upwards of three thousand,' Sam replied. 'You'd most likely heard of us from our horses, though. Chisolm Chief is one of our studs.'

The marshal raised a hand. 'That's where I heard the name! Lester Magnuson over by Laramie won't use a stud if it ain't outa Chisolm Chief.'

'I've met him,' Sam confirmed. 'Small man. Wears a mustache pertneart as big as yours.'

The marshal grinned, stroking his very striking facial feature. 'Pertneart as big, but not near as fine and handsome a mustache, though, wouldn't you agree?'

Sam grinned in response, taking refuge in his own cup of coffee. 'I won't take sides,' he dodged. 'I wouldn't wanta offend one of the boss's best customers.'

'So what brings you clear to Wyoming?'

'Horse thieves.'

The marshal's eyebrows shot up again. 'Horse thieves?'

Sam nodded. 'Someone stole a bunch of our horses, along with some from three of our neighbors. I tracked 'em north.'

'You find 'em?'

'I found 'em. Four of 'em.'

The marshal simply sipped his coffee, staring at Sam, waiting silently for a lot more information than that.

Sam decided to comply. 'I caught up with 'em over at Hinsmeyer's Mill Iron.'

When he offered nothing further, the marshal pursued it. 'You call 'em out?'

'I called 'em horse thieves.'

'Hinsmeyer and his boys back your play?'

'They would've if I'd needed it. Things happened sorta fast. I had to go ahead and empty their saddles afore Hinsmeyer's hands had a chance to get in on it.'

The marshal stared hard at him for a long moment. 'You took on all four of 'em by yourself?'

Sam shrugged and took another drink of his coffee. 'Only three at once. The ringleader made a dumb play by himself when he figured out we was gonna take a good look at his bills o' sale.'

'Are you really that fast with a gun?'

'He's really that fast with a gun,' Kate replied across her own coffee cup. 'One of Lance Russell's gunmen drew on him the other day. He didn't have a chance.'

The marshal studied Kate, betraying the fact that she had mentioned something of greater importance than the stolen horses. 'You saw him shoot Texas Tom?'

'I saw him shoot one of Russell's hired gunmen. I don't have any idea what his name was. Why?'

The marshal looked back and forth between Kate and Sam, studying them carefully. 'The story I got was that Texas Tom was shot in cold blood by a drifter.'

Kate snorted. 'That's the biggest lie I've ever heard in my life. Lance Russell and two of his hired guns tried to force me to sell out to him for five hundred dollars. He threatened to turn his hired guns on me right in front of my son until I agreed. If Sam hadn't been here, I don't know what I would have done.'

Denton looked at Sam. 'They didn't see you?'

'Not then. I was out back cuttin' wood. That's why I was hangin' around here. I offered to cut Kate a wood pile for winter in exchange for a few days' good grass for the horses. I wanted to fatten 'em up some before I headed south with 'em.'

'So they didn't see you?'

'Not then. I was listenin', though. When things started gettin' ugly, I stepped around the corner. I ordered 'em off the place. One of 'em decided he'd poke a little daylight through me instead. He wasn't nowhere's near fast enough.'

'Not too common, a gun hand willin' to swing an axe.'

'I'm not a gun hand. I'm just a workin' cowboy that happens to be handy with a gun. I'd just as soon never have to pull it on anybody. I don't hire my gun out.'

'What happened up along Buffalo Ridge?' the marshal asked abruptly.

Billy piped up with the answer. All three of the adults had forgotten his presence, intent as they were on their conversation.

'I get to tell 'bout that! Some guys what was a-stealin' a whole bunch of our cows. Me'n Ma and Sam seen the tracks where they'd rounded up a whole bunch. We followed 'em. We caught up with 'em, but Ma and Sam wouldn't let me help. I had my rifle too, but they wouldn't let me do nothin'. They made me stay with the horses. They shot two o' the rustlers, then made the other three walk without their boots. I bet their feet was plumb sore afore they got where they was goin'.'

Denton pursed his lips carefully. 'Well, that's either the straight of it, or you did a real fine job teachin' the boy a tall tale.'

'I ain't lyin', mister! Ask my ma.'

'I believe you, son,' the marshal assured him. 'Your story makes a lot more sense than the one I got from Russell.' He turned to Sam. 'You know Ben Grede?'

'Never met him.'

'I know him,' Kate interjected. 'He runs that saloon and gambling hall and house of ill repute in Mariposa. He's bought out three or four ranchers and homesteaders. I wouldn't trust him as far as I could throw him. He's as hungry for more land as Russell is, but he hasn't bothered me. Why?'

'Him and Russell swore out a complaint against you, Sam. They swore it out together. Said you been rag-tailin' their outfits and causin' all sorts o' trouble.'

'I ain't done one dad-gummed thing against the law,' Sam retorted. 'If they wanta claim I have, let 'em ride out here and say it to my face.'

'They rode clear down to Laramie to swear out a complaint?' Kate demanded.

Denton stroked his mustache. 'Well,

no, not exactly. I just happened to be ridin' up this way on some other business. Russell spotted me when I stopped by Grede's place for a beer. They told me all about what a real bad hardcase this Sam Heller is, and how it's my duty to rid the country of such as him. I told 'em I'd look into it. Near as I can tell, you folks are the ones that need to watch your backs.'

Sam's eyes continued to flash fire. 'Russell knows where I stand, and what he can do about it any time he wants. I'll have a little chat with Grede.'

Denton acted as if he wanted to take exception to the statement, then finished his coffee instead. 'Just make sure you stay within the law,' he said. 'Don't give 'em anything they can use to make me take sides.'

Sam was already mapping out a course of action in his mind he was sure the marshal would not approve.

9

The moon hung in the clear sky, bathing the earth in soft light. The harshness of the day's heat had given way to a surprising chill. Far distant, the soft cry of an owl sounded like a lullaby of peace to all but the rodents it sought.

Sam stood in the deep shadows of a grove of trees. He studied the area ahead of him intently. He was in no hurry, he had time to be sure who was where, and why.

He had entered Mariposa without using the road, keeping to the bottoms of draws, skirting hills, staying well out of sight. His horse was just beyond a clump of plum bushes, tied to a small elm tree.

In front of him the back side of Grede's Lucky Lady Saloon and Gambling Hall spilled yellow light from every window. From his vantage he could see through clearly, watching the lively business within.

He had quickly picked out which windows opened into Grede's living quarters. The windows were larger, the drapes that hung on the inside of those windows were plush fabric. The visible furnishings within were elaborate and clearly top quality. Every facet of those quarters reeked of prosperity.

As far as he had been able to ascertain, there was only one guard on this side of the building. Either Grede was supremely confident, or thought he had no enemies likely to be stalking him. That didn't square with the mental image Sam had formed of the man.

Grede himself seemed to be alone in his quarters. He was seated at a desk, with several ledgers open in front of him. The window behind him was open to the world. 'He either thinks he ain't got an enemy in the world or he's dumber'n a knot-headed calf,' Sam muttered to himself.

The lone guard idled at the corner of the building, leaning against it, listening to the noise of the conversations and revelry within. He rolled a cigarette and smoked it, oblivious to the fact that he was broadcasting his location to anyone approaching.

The whole scene made no sense to him, but he finally decided he had to accept it at face value. He made a wide, silent circle, coming up on the guard from around the corner he lounged beside. He stood there, less than three feet from him, watching his shadow. When the shadow indicated he had turned to look along the back side of the building, Sam stepped into the open. The guard sensed his presence just in time to turn into the gun barrel that slammed into the side of his head. He crumpled noiselessly to the ground.

Moving swiftly and soundlessly, Sam approached the open window. He stepped over the sill and eased himself into the room, almost within reach of Ben Grede. The saloon keeper gave no indication he sensed Sam's presence.

Sam stood still in indecision. He looked around. Just to his right a wingback chair, upholstered in rich burgundy velvet, stood empty. He eased himself into it, holding his gun in his lap. He lifted his right boot on to his left knee in an exaggerated position of relaxation. By doing so, he knew he also concealed the gun from Grede's angle.

'Nice night,' he said, keeping his voice conversational.

Grede jumped as if he had been shot. He whirled, nearly upsetting his chair. 'Who are you? How'd you get in here?'

'I walked. My name's Sam Heller.'

Recognition flashed in Grede's eyes, followed by a perceptible paling of his face. 'The gunman.'

'Only when I have to be,' Sam rejoined amicably. 'I understand you've sworn out a complaint against me with the US marshal.'

A film that should have been invisible passed over Grede's eyes. Sam recognized it for the wariness he expected. 'I went along with Lance's complaint,' he admitted. 'You killed a couple of his boys.'

'Did he tell you why?'

'Because he wants the widow's place.'

'Because his boys were busy drivin' off about fifty head of her cows.'

Grede's eyebrows shot up. 'They were rustlin'?'

'That's what it was called the last I knew.'

'You got any proof of that?'

'The woman and her son were both with me. She shot one of 'em.'

'The Bond woman shot one of Lance's hands?'

'She shot one of the rustlers. You're the one that seems to know it was Russell's hands that were doing the rustling.'

Grede laughed unexpectedly. 'He sure didn't tell me that one of his tough Texas gun hands got himself shot by a woman.'

'She'd have shot the one at her place a couple days before that if I hadn't done it first.'

Grede's smile disappeared. 'You shot another one of his hands?'

'I shot one that drew on me. Russell thought he could force her to sell out to him for five hundred dollars, lock, stock, and barrel. He doesn't seem to have much respect for a woman.'

Grede took a deep breath. 'I'll give you that. That bothers me some about Lance. I got more respect for the whores that work for me than he does for good women.'

'So what are your intentions toward her?' Sam demanded.

'I'd love to buy her place, if she wants to sell it.'

'For five hundred dollars, I suppose.'

Grede shook his head. 'I said I'd love to buy it, not steal it. I might not be the most respectable citizen of Mariposa, but I'm not that low, to take advantage of a widow. By the way, where's my guard? Did you come in that window?'

'I did. Your guard's right where he was. When he wakes up, he'll have a dandy headache.'

Grede thought about it a long moment, then nodded. 'You know I could holler and have half a dozen of my men in here instantly, don't you?'

'You know you'd be dead before the first one made it through the door, don't you?'

Grede studied him a long moment. 'I like you. Do you want a job?'

'I got one. I just want to know whether I'm gonna have to deal with you to make sure the Bond woman gets a fair shake.'

Grede shook his head. 'Like I said, I'd love to have her place. But I play it straight up with everyone. I don't need to be crooked or lowdown to make money. I probably made more money this year than you've ever seen at one time. But I've done it honest. I don't rig the games. I don't water the whiskey. And I don't let the girls roll any drunk cowboys. If the Bond woman wants to sell out, I'll pay her a fair price for her patent and market price for her livestock, whenever she wants to sell.'

It was Sam's turn to study the other man for a long moment. He stood up and dropped his gun back into its holster. 'Fair enough,' he said.

He deliberately turned his back on Grede, knowing he was inviting a bullet in the back if he had mis-read the man. How badly he had mis-read the man became immediately apparent.

'You'd best not be goin' out that window.'

He looked back at the owner of the Lucky Lady. 'Why not?'

'You don't really think I'd sit there with my back to a window, with the lamps on, without taking measures to be sure I don't get shot, do you?'

Sam's mind cast about feverishly, trying to figure out what he might have missed. Either Grede was bluffing, or he had missed something that could well be fatal. 'It sure enough appears that way,' he stalled.

Grede chuckled. 'Every fifteen minutes my guards have to check in. When the guard you knocked out didn't, someone came to check on him. By now there's half a dozen men with their guns trained on you. If I give the signal, you're a dead man. And it doesn't matter how fast or good you are. You're standing in good lamplight. My boys are standing in the dark. You don't have a chance to see them. They don't have a chance of missing you.'

If it was a bluff, it was a good one. It explained why Grede was so willing to visit. He was giving his men time to get into position. Now the tables were turned, and Sam was in a situation from which he had no chance to escape.

He thought of the bustling saloon and casino on the other side of the door. If he took Grede hostage and exited that way, he might make it to the outside door alive.

Grede chuckled as if reading his thoughts. 'You don't need to try to take me hostage,' he said. 'I already said I like you.'

He picked up the coal oil lamp from

his desk, walked to the window, and swung it back and forth twice in a wide arc. He set it back on the desk. 'You can go ahead and leave now. The next time you stop in to visit, please use the front door.'

Sam hesitated for a long moment, uncertain whether to take the man's word. He shrugged inwardly, deciding it was as good a course of action as any. He stepped out through the window. To his left, the guard he had knocked out was struggling to his feet. He walked over to him and grabbed his arm, steadying him. He steered him toward the open window. 'Better go tell your boss you got a headache,' he advised.

The guard shook his head and tried to focus his eyes on whomever had helped him up. There was nobody there.

10

The angry whine past his right ear needed no explanation. Sam dived for cover, even as he heard the 'thwack' of a bullet burying itself in the back of the house.

Whipping his .45 from its holster where it hung near at hand, he took cover behind a large tree. With some subconscious part of his mind, he had already aligned the whine of the leaden missile of death with the sound of its impact on the house, and knew the approximate location of his hidden adversary.

Standing gun in hand, braced with his bare back against the rough bark of the tree, he listened intently. There was only silence for a long moment, then he heard faint whispering from the copse of trees that reached nearest to Kate's ranch house.

'Did I git 'im?'

'I don't know. C'mon. Let's just get outa here.'

Even in their whispers, the slur in their voices and lack of reasoning ability testified to the amount of courage they had drunk on their way there. 'I ain't leavin' till I know I killed that worthless coyote what cost me my job.'

'You can't just shoot 'im down like a dog.'

'I sure can't call 'im out in a stand-up fight. You seen him handle that gun?'

'If you kill 'im this way, they'll hang you.'

'Not if they can't find me. We're headin' outa the country soon's I take care of him.'

Sam eyed his surroundings carefully. If he had their location fixed accurately in his mind, he should be able to crouch below the level of the wood pile, scurry around the corner of the house, then approach the hidden pair from an unexpected direction.

Without hesitation he silently lifted

his gunbelt and holster from their perch and slid the .45 into its holster. Careful to stay behind the tree's massive trunk, he strapped the belt and holster around him, then fastened the strap to keep the weapon from falling out. He dropped to all fours and scuttled swiftly past the wood pile and around the corner of the house.

Ducking down, he paused to listen. No sound indicated his intended killers had noted his departure from where they thought him either pinned down or dead.

Kate stepped out of the door. She looked at Sam with a mixture of concern and fear. 'Did I hear a gunshot?'

Sam put his finger to his mouth to shush her. 'Stay inside,' he cautioned in a soft voice, knowing a soft voice would actually carry less than a hissed whisper.

'Couple fellas snuck up behind the house and took a shot at me. I'm gonna circle around and switch the surprise some.'

Kate frowned. In scarcely more than a whisper, she asked, 'Who is it?'

He shook his head. 'Not sure. I'm guessin' it's that Farmer kid. Hiram said he was gonna can 'im. I'm guessin' he stopped by to get even before he pulls freight.'

'You think it's Bobby? What are you going to do?'

'That all depends on him. Just stay in the house. Keep your rifle handy, in case it's one of them that comes around after it's over, instead of me.'

Without waiting for a response, he moved to the other corner of the house. Looking around it carefully, he mapped out in his mind a path of movement that would keep him concealed from his attackers. Without hesitance he followed that path as swiftly and silently as he could.

Once in the neck of timber, he moved more slowly but more confidently. Placing each foot carefully, so as not to betray his presence, he circled the pair, coming up within thirty feet of them without either one being aware of his approach.

'You boys lookin' for me?'

The effect of his voice was electric. One of the men leaped up with a shriek, thrusting his hands as high as he could reach into the air. The other whirled, pistol in hand, toward the surprising location of his intended prey. Before he could focus on Sam, however, a hurtling hunk of lead from Sam's .45 drove him backward. He sprawled across the downed tree he had been using for cover and to steady his gun, dead before he slid on downward and toppled sideways.

'Don't shoot! Don't shoot!' the other man pleaded, his voice suddenly sounding markedly more sober than the slurred whispers Sam had heard. 'I done tried my best to talk 'im outa comin' after you. I didn't want no part o' this. Honest. I ain't got no bone to pick with you. Honest, Mister. Don't shoot me.'

'Who are you?' Sam demanded, the

harshness of his voice making the other wince.

'My name's Younger. Fred Younger. I been Bobby's friend on the H Bar V. He talked me into headin' down to Texas with him, when Hi canned him. We hung around town for a week, an' he just kept gettin' madder'n madder. But I didn't know nothin' 'bout him aimin' to back-shoot you afore he left the country, or I wouldn'ta gone with him. Honest. I ain't no back-shooter. And you gotta believe I wouldn'ta never let 'im do what he said he was gonna do to the Bond Widder. I wouldn't let even my best friend rape nobody. Honest. I just wouldn'ta stood still for that atall.'

Sam hesitated a long moment, then said, 'Unbuckle your gunbelt and let it drop.'

Moving as if his life depended on his haste, Younger complied. 'Now let's go get you boys' horses.'

'What . . . what're you gonna do?'

'You're gonna put your friend across his horse and haul him to town. Then

I'm gonna let you ride outa this country in one piece. But if I ever see you hangin' around these parts again, I'll kill you on sight.'

Relief flooded Younger's face. 'Thanks, Mister! You won't be sorry. I ain't never . . . I mean I wouldn't never . . . I mean — '

'The horses!' Sam interrupted.

'Yes sir!'

In other circumstances, his combination of running and stumbling drunkenly might have been funny. As it was, it only angered Sam further. Younger retraced his earlier steps and returned leading both his and Farmer's horses. By the time he reached them, Sam was where he could watch to be sure he didn't try to pull either rifle from its scabbard. Younger never so much as glanced at the weapons, hurrying as fast as his inebriated state would allow, to comply with Sam's commands.

Grunting, sweating profusely and straining, he heaved his friend's body across the saddle and lashed it into place. He started to mount, then turned back toward Sam. He scratched his head behind and above his right ear, knocking his hat askew without seeming to notice. 'Uh, I know I ain't got no right to ask this, but that there gun an' holster set me back a couple months' wages. If I dump the shells out've it, do you reckon you could see your way clear to let me take it with me? I didn't have much money comin' from Hi when we turned in our time, and I done drunk up most o' that the past week. I just flat ain't got enough money to get me another one.'

Sam considered it a long moment. The harsh lines relaxed around his mouth. 'Get it.'

Once again, relief flooded Younger's face. The fleeting thought crossed Sam's mind that the cowboy would be a pushover in a poker game. Every thought in his head could be clearly read in his face. 'Thanks, Mister. You're a real stand-up guy. I really appreciate this. I'll find a way to pay you back someday, if I can.'

He picked up his gunbelt and strapped it around his waist. He almost toppled over when he lifted one foot into the stirrup, but managed to grasp the saddle horn and haul himself into the saddle. Once in the saddle, he sat as if it were second nature, in spite of the whiskey he had consumed. Gripping the reins of Farmer's mount, he rode away at a fast trot.

'Are you sure that was a good idea?'

Sam whirled, his gun pointing at the surprising voice as if of its own volition. He jerked the gun aside violently, almost yelling at Kate. 'Don't ever come up behind me that way!'

Shock and surprise registered on her face, but relaxed as soon as he had swung the gun away and holstered it. 'I'm sorry,' she apologized. 'I got worried, because I heard one shot, then nothing more. Was it Bobby?'

He nodded. 'Him and a friend of his, that he got drunk then roped into comin' along with 'im.'

'Are you sure it was a good idea to give him his gun back?' she asked again.

Sam shrugged. 'I don't think he's any threat. Even when they didn't think I could hear 'em, he was tryin' to talk Bobby into leavin'. He just let a bad guy use friendship to rope 'im into bein' where he didn't wanta be. Even then, I think Bobby had to get 'im good and drunk to get him to go along this far.'

'He told you that?'

'That, and other things.'

Her face mirrored her confusion. 'Other things? What other things?'

'It don't matter.'

The confusion changed to determination in her face instantly. 'It matters if it concerns me.'

'It don't need to concern you now.'

She threw her rifle on the ground and stamped her foot in exasperation. 'Don't you start trying to treat me like a dumb and helpless woman! I want to know what other things you meant. Tell me!'

It was Sam's turn to have uncertainty telegraphed on his face. He hesitated a long moment, then said, 'He said that no matter how drunk he was, he wasn't going to let Bobby do what he had in mind with you.'

Her face paled with understanding of what he was saying. Almost at once the pallor was erased by the red flush of anger. 'He thought all he had to do was get rid of you, and then he could do whatever he wanted with me? Is that what you think too? Do you think I'm just a helpless dumb widow? Listen! I do not need you to take care of me, Sam Heller! I am perfectly capable of taking care of myself, and I will take care of myself just as soon as you take those stupid horses of yours and ride out of my life.'

Her anger was reflected in his own face at once, masking the hurt her words had inflicted. The anger gave his response a much harsher edge than he intended. 'I just might do that.'

'Then you just go ahead and do that!

And the sooner the better. If you want paying for the wood you've chopped and the men you've shot, I'll find the money to pay you.'

'I ain't never asked a dime from you, and I don't want your money.'

'You haven't asked for anything else either, and it's a good thing, because there's nothing else for you here either. The sooner you're out of my life and Billy's the better it'll be for both of us.'

'If that's the way you feel about it, I'll pack my stuff and be on my way within the hour.'

'Fine! I'll fix you a lunch to take so you won't have to slow down until you're clear out of the country.'

'If I need a lunch I'll fix it myself. I don't need anything from you any more'n you need me.'

'So throw it away if you want to, but you're not leaving without something to eat in your saddle-bag.'

With that she scooped up her rifle and stamped away to the house. With equal anger boiling within him, he walked swiftly to where his bedroll remained spread under a large oak tree. In minutes he had his belongings gathered, his bedroll tied behind his saddle, and was ready to ride.

He had waited only scarce minutes when Kate appeared with a cloth bag, tied securely with a piece of rawhide. She almost threw it at him, rather than handing it. 'Here's some food,' she said, her voice still quivering with anger. 'I thank you for all your help and for the wood you've chopped. Billy and I will be just fine for the winter now.'

Sam tried to soften the hard edges of her anger. 'Uh, Hiram said him and the boys would sorta keep an eye on your cattle.'

Her anger flared hot again. 'Sam Heller, how many times do I have to tell you I don't need you, I don't need Hiram and Eduardo and Bart, and I don't need sympathy! Billy and I will manage just fine. Now get off my place!'

Even in her anger, Sam thought she was the most beautiful creature he had ever seen. He fought down the urge to reach past her anger and sweep her into his arms. He could almost taste the sweetness of her lips, feel the shape of her body against him.

Instead he stepped into the saddle and jammed his spurs into his horse's side, riding away at a canter.

Minutes later he tried to explain to Billy.

'You can't leave, Sam! Me an' Ma, we need you here!'

Sam shook his head. 'Your ma doesn't want me here.'

'Yes she does! She ain't smiled or laughed since Pa got killed, till you came. She even joked about it when her an' me had to leave the house so you could take a hot bath with that good-smellin' soap Ma makes. She really wants you to stay.'

The smell of that soap wafted across his memory like the grasping tentacles of some irresistible creature. It was the same smell he caught wisps of whenever he was close to Kate. She made the softest, best smelling soap he had ever used. He had never bathed as often as he had in his brief stay here.

He shook his head to rinse the thoughts from his mind. 'I can't stay, Billy. I've helped where I can. I got to get these horses back to my boss and the other ranches they was stolen from. You and your ma will be just fine.'

Billy fought in vain to keep the tears from his eyes. 'You'll come back, won't you? After you get the horses took home, you'll come back? Promise me you'll come back, Sam!'

Sam fought against his own emotions. 'I can't promise, Billy.'

'Promise me you'll try, at least.'

Sam sighed heavily. 'I'll see,' he evaded.

'You gotta come back, Sam. You just gotta.'

Sam reined his horse away, gathered his small remuda into a bunch and started moving them south. The last words that rang in his head reached him, carried distantly on the wind, from a young boy standing clear up on top of his saddle, his hands cupped around his mouth to shout as loud as he could. 'Please come back, Sam! Please? Please?'

11

Anger still boiling within him kept Sam Heller's lips a thin, straight line. He had pushed the horses harder than necessary, taking out his anger and frustration on them. The quiet voice in the back of his mind, nagging that they didn't deserve that, only heightened and maintained his anger.

The large corral behind the livery barn in Mariposa stood open and ready. He hazed the horses into it, then swung down and shut the gate. The hostler ambled out as he turned to lead his horse into the stable. 'Puttin' 'em up overnight?'

Sam resisted the urge to say, 'No, I just wanted to practice corralling them.' Instead he asked, 'How much?'

'Ten cents a head, unless you want 'em grained.'

'Just hay'll be enough. There's twenty

one of 'em. I'll be wantin' this one grained and rubbed down, though.'

The hostler totted up the sum in his head. 'That'll come to two fifty.'

'Want me to pay you now?'

The hostler shrugged. 'Suit yourself.'

'Just as well,' Sam said, reaching past the belt of his chaps to dig the money from his pants pocket. He counted out the money that disappeared into the hostler's pocket. 'I'll likely be pullin' out about first light.'

'I bed in the room at the back. Whistle if you need anything.'

Without answering, Sam strode out the front door of the livery barn and headed down the main street of Mariposa. He wouldn't have needed to stop over in town on his way, but it was one night he wouldn't need to keep the small remuda together while he tried to catch what sleep he could.

He stepped through the front door of the Lucky Lady Saloon and stopped dead in his tracks. It looked at first as if some sideshow from a traveling circus had come to town. Everyone at both the bar and the various gaming tables had stopped what they were doing. Every eye was fixed on the entertainment at the bar.

Several of Ben Grede's private security force were lounging near the bar, grinning broadly. One of their own was loudly mocking Bart Spalding's stutter. The son of the H Bar V rancher stood red-faced with anger. His fists knotted and unknotted at his side. Once in a while he glanced at the half-circle of his antagonist's friends, as if weighing his chances against the lot of them.

The burly leader of the mockery leered at the hesitant cowboy. 'Wh-wh-wh-what's the m-m-m-matter, B-B-B-B-Bartholomew? The c-c-c-cat got your t-t-t-t-tongue?'

Something exploded in Sam's head. Anger and frustration had been boiling inside him ever since he had words with Kate, gathered his horses and left. Helplessness and lack of understanding of what had even led to the quarrel had only deepened his dark mood. The loneliness he refused to admit feeling already brought that mood to a boiling point. Seeing the arrogance of the burly bouncer mocking the Spalding boy's speech problem released the trigger. Sam snapped.

Without a word he strode forward. With no hesitation or warning, his left fist slammed into the burly man's mouth. Teeth escaped their roots, two of them flying clear into the back of the man's throat, causing him to swallow them instantly; blood flew from his face as if a ripe tomato had been smashed. The left to the mouth was followed instantly by a right hook to his left ear that guaranteed he would sport a cauliflowered ear the rest of his life. A left uppercut knocked his chin upward just in time for the right that followed it to connect solidly with the point of his chin. The big man toppled backward, unconscious, to sprawl in the sawdust that covered the floor.

There was an instant of incredulous calm, then the half-circle of his friends rushed forward as one to overwhelm this newcomer who had dared to attack one of their own.

Years of frustration and anger had been building in Bartholomew Spalding; Sam's wordless actions seemed to release a spring within him as well. As the friends of the downed bouncer rushed forward, the first three were met by a huge arm, swinging with the size and force of a tree limb. All three were swept backward. Their feet were well above their heads by the time their heads contacted the sawdust that cradled their friend. At least two chairs from nearby tables were reduced to kindling beneath them.

Before they hit the floor, Sam had already stepped forward and met the closest of his attackers with a swift knee to the groin, followed by another knee to the face that lowered accommodatingly as the man doubled forward in pain. To enforce the second knee's impact, Sam had grabbed a handful of hair and helped the head propel itself into his rising knee. Like the first man, he was unconscious before he crumpled on the floor.

With a roar of released rage, Bart grabbed the belt of another of the attackers and hauled him off his feet. Swinging him in a circle high above his head, he threw him like a rag doll into the mass of bodies surging forward. Four men were carried backward by the weight and force of more than two hundred pounds of flesh and bone hurtling into them. A table and two more chairs fell victim to the burden they were not built to bear.

Unseen, with the first noise of the brawl, Ben Grede rushed out of the door of his office. He stepped to the back end of the bar and engaged in a hurried conversation with the bartender. Grede held out his hand to the bartender, who reached under the bar and retrieved a sawn-off double-barreled twelve gauge shotgun.

Others of Grede's security force from every quarter of the saloon and gambling hall were already rushing to their fellows' aid. Fighting fiercely side by side, it was obvious that Sam and Bart would soon be overwhelmed by sheer force of numbers. The only thing that had delayed that inevitable event this long, was the difficulty the bouncers' reinforcements were having stepping over and around the growing pile of their downed friends.

Over and above the din of the raging battle, the roar of the twelve gauge echoed from the ceiling and walls, making the chandeliers quiver. The noise level dropped abruptly but not entirely. A second round from the shotgun, fired into the floor, brought everything to a sudden halt. All eyes turned to the owner, glaring over the cigar clamped tightly in the corner of his mouth.

Grede jabbed a finger at one of his men closest to him. 'You! Frank! Get a couple of these idiots to help you, and haul Lyle out of here and throw him in a horse tank. When you get him woke up, tell him I said to turn in his time and get out of town. I hire you boys to keep things quiet and peaceable around here, not to start fights.'

He waited a pregnant moment to let his words soak in, then continued. 'The rest of you, give a listen.'

He pointed to Bart Spalding. 'This boy is welcome in this place any time he wants to stop in, and there's a free drink waiting for him any time he does. And the first one of you I hear makin' fun of him will answer to me.'

Again he glared at his crew of enforcers, giving his words time to penetrate even the thickest of skulls. Then he addressed the chagrined group again. 'Do you all understand that?'

Nobody responded. They all studied their boots intently.

Grede's voice raised an octave, as did the volume of his question. 'I said, Do you all understand that?'

Instantly his words were met by a

chorus of mumbled compliance and nodding heads.

Whirling, Grede tossed the now empty shotgun back to the bartender and disappeared into his office.

Deathly silence descended on the entire establishment. It was the bartender who spoke up. 'Well, what are you all waiting for? The show's over. Go back to what you were doing.'

He turned to Sam and Bart. 'What can I get for you boys? It's on the house.'

Bart studied the blood on his skinned up knuckles, as he had never seen them in that state before. He looked at Sam, then at the bartender. 'Uh, yeah. Yeah. I could use a drink.'

Sam grinned at him. 'You give a pretty good account of yourself for a kid,' he offered.

Bart grinned back, suddenly feeling euphoric and not understanding why. 'I ain't never done nothin' about folks makin' fun of me before. That felt good. That felt plumb good!'

Sam refrained from commenting that the young man had made the statement without any hint of a stutter.

Over the next hour they talked. Mostly, Sam talked to drown out the echo of Kate's words that ripped his guts apart every time he remembered them. Every time the conversation lagged, the words repeated themselves in his mind. 'I don't need you, Sam Heller, and I don't need sympathy! Billy and I will manage just fine. Now get off my place!'

Even in his mind, he couldn't stand to listen. To silence their unbearable pain, he talked to Bart. Sam told him about the ranch he worked for in the Indian Nation, its location, the crew, how it felt to work there, and experiences he had doing so. He had no idea the conversation would affect the rest of his life.

12

Dust hung in the still air. It was hot for early November. Sam Heller hazed the last of the steers into the shipping corral and swiped the sweat from his face with his shirt sleeve.

'Bath's gonna feel good tonight,' he muttered to himself.

Instantly he wished he hadn't said that — or thought it. Once again, as for countless other times, he fought down the thought of the shrinking bar of soap he had carefully hoarded. In his mind he could smell it already. Smelling it, he smelled Kate as well. The familiar ache knotted his stomach and twisted barbed wire around his heart.

He gritted his teeth and shook his head, feeling the sand grate between his teeth as he did so. As hard as he fought not to, he heard again the plaintive cry, borne on the breeze, 'Please come back, Sam! Please?'

He jerked his horse's head around sharply and rammed his spurs into the startled animal's sides. The horse lunged forward, even as the spurs sent sharp pains stabbing into Sam's conscience. 'He didn't deserve that,' his conscience nagged him.

'You OK, Sam?' Oz Maquire asked, loping up alongside him.

'I'm fine!' Sam fired back at his friend. 'Let's go home.'

He slowed his horse to a walk as Oz fell in beside him. 'Thinkin' about her again, huh?'

Several angry retorts fought against each other to be first released. Stifling them all, Sam sighed heavily. Instead of the first half dozen things that came to mind, he said, 'You'd think I'd stop moonin' about her and get on with things, wouldn't you? It's been over a month.'

'You thought about goin' back?'

Silence hung between the two close

friends for a quarter of a mile. When Oz had nearly forgotten the question, Sam said, 'It wouldn't work. She's the one that told me to hit the trail.'

Oz shook his head. 'Yeah, but do you think she meant it?'

'Why would she say it, if she didn't mean it?'

'She's a woman.'

'I was well aware of that. What's that got to do with anything?'

'Everything. Women are like that. They say all sorts of stuff they don't mean when they get mad. Then they get done bein' mad, they act like they never said it, and then they expect a fella to forget they said it too.'

Sam shook his head. 'I ain't built like that. Things like that ain't that easy to forget.'

'She ain't either, I notice.'

Sam shot Oz a look that indicated his friend was treading dangerously close to forbidden ground, but he didn't answer.

They were within a mile of the Rafter

J headquarters when both of their heads jerked up. As one, they spotted a small cloud of dust. 'Somethin's up,' Oz warned.

'One rider,' Sam responded.

'Hurryin' some.'

'Wearin' out a horse for sure.'

'Your trouble or mine, you reckon?'

Sam shrugged. 'Hard to tell. Hope it ain't nothin' big. I'm tired.'

'Me too. That last bunch of steers were plumb ringy.'

The distant cloud of dust grew steadily closer. Both men studied it. 'Anyone you know?' Oz asked.

Sam frowned. 'Looks like a guy I know, but it couldn't be him. He's up in Wyoming.'

'If it's him, I hope he ain't run his horse like that the whole way.'

'If he had, he'd have a dead horse. He's a big man.'

'Well, it's a big man all right.'

Sam's frown deepened. He swore. 'It sure looks like him. C'mon.'

He touched his spurs to his horse

and lifted to a canter, speeding their meeting with the mystery rider heading their way. Oz kept pace, glancing sideways at his friend with growing concern as he saw the question give way to certainty in Sam's face.

It was only minutes later when Bartholomew Spalding reined in his spent and panting horse beside them. His words tumbled out as fast as he could force them. 'Sam, you gotta get back there. Kate needs you. Russell's finally figured out you ain't there protectin' her no more. He's up to somethin' and he's hirin' on gun hands an' everything. He acts like he's gettin' ready to take on the whole country if he has to, to get that place o' hers. Pa an' Eddie'll do all they can to keep him from it, but they can't hold 'em off for long. Some of our hands are willin' to jump in too, but not all of 'em. Some of 'em are just plumb scared, 'specially when Russell's bringin' in all them hardcases. You just gotta come back, Sam.'

'Kate doesn't want me,' Sam responded, his voice much harsher than he intended.

Bart shook his head emphatically. 'That there just ain't so, Sam. Kate, she can't hardly even talk to nobody without bawlin' no more. I ain't seen her since you left without her eyes bein' all red an' swelled up, like she's been bawlin' most o' the time. Billy, he just sits around all the time, lookin' like he lost his best friend. They ain't sayin' nothin', on account o' they get all weepy when they try to, but they're both awantin' you there somethin' awful. And not just to protect 'em, neither. That there woman, she's just plumb head over heels in love with you, Sam. That's what my Ma says, an' she's a Mexican, you know. Mexicans, they understand stuff like that.'

'You rode all the way down here just to tell me that?'

'No, I rode all the way down here to find you and haul you back up there where you belong.'

'How'd you find me?'

'You told me where the ranch was, after we whupped up on them boys o' Grede's, remember?'

Sam sighed heavily. 'Sometimes I talk too much.'

'Well, you're talkin' too much now,' Bart agreed. 'You need to be grabbin' your stuff so we can hit the road back to Wyoming.'

'How long did it take you to get here?'

'Two days.'

'Two days? Didn't you stop to eat or sleep?'

'Nope. We ain't got that much time. I'd ride a horse till he was pertneart ready to drop, then I'd stop at a ranch and swap horses and keep headin' south. I 'spect we can swap horses at the same places on the way back, an' we can be there day after tomorrow.'

'That'd put you four days in the saddle without sleep.'

'That don't matter none. What matters is that we get back there afore it's too late.

'You forgot to stutter. What happened to your stutter?'

Bart grinned. 'I d-d-don't hardly stutter no more, 'cept when I'm thinkin' about it.'

Oz spoke up for the first time. 'I'll go collect your time from Hap while you're gettin' your stuff together,' he offered.

Sam jerked his attention to his friend. 'I ain't even said I was gonna go.'

'You don't need to. You're goin'. You know it. I know it. You're headin' to Wyoming, and you ain't never comin' back to the Indian Nation. That's just how it is.'

Sam glared at him a long moment before his look softened. 'You comin' with me?'

Oz pursed his lips thoughfully. 'I just might do that,' he said.

'We could sure use you,' Sam said, surprised at the gratitude and relief he heard in his own voice.

Bart's face lit up as if the sun had just come out from under a cloud. 'You mean you're comin'? You're really gonna come back with me? Eeeeehah!'

Bart threw his hat as high up in the air as he could throw it, causing his horse to shy and sidestep nervously. 'You're gonna spook your horse,' Sam scolded.

Bart grinned. 'Aw, he's too tired to spook much. He's just about at the end of his rope. He needs a good rubdown an' a bait of oats before he'd have energy enough to shy very hard.'

Sam returned the infectious grin of the youngster. 'Oh, by the way, Oz, this here's Bart Spalding. His family runs the H Bar V up in Wyoming. Bart, this is Oz Maguire. We been friends a while.'

Oz maneuvered his horse over where he could reach Bart, and held out a hand. 'Bart, glad to meet you. Sam told me about you playin' nine-pins with them fellas in the saloon.'

Bart frowned. 'What's nine-pins?'

'Oh, that's a game where you take a heavy ball and roll it into wooden pins standin' up a ways off, and see how many you can knock over.'

'Oh.' Bart's frown turned into another grin. 'Yeah, I guess I did sorta do that, didn't I?'

Sam lifted his reins impatiently. 'If gettin' back there is all that important, we'd best stop sittin' here chinnin' and get ready to hit the trail.'

As one they turned their horses toward the Rafter J, each lost in his own thoughts of what lay ahead.

13

'Looks quiet.'

'Too quiet. The cattle we seen on the way in ain't been bothered. The place looks normal. Nobody nosin' around.'

'You're sure Russell's up to somethin', are you?'

'All indications sure been pointin' thataway.'

Sam, Bart Spalding and Oz Maguire sat their exhausted horses, looking down from a long ridge on to the site of Kate Bond's ranch yard.

'So what do we do now?' Oz wondered.

Sam took in a deep breath. 'Well, it looks like things are calm enough here. There ain't no need to let them know I'm in the country.'

'You ain't gonna tell Kate you're here?'

He shook his head. His lips were a

thin, hard line beneath the coating of trail dust. 'She don't want anything to do with me. She made that real plain.'

'Women say lots o' things they don't mean.'

'They mean lots o' the things they say, too. She didn't leave no room for doubt. She don't never wanta see me again.'

'The boy don't likely feel that way.'

'I ain't his say-so.'

Bart cleared his throat. 'Like I think I tol' you down there in the Indian Nation, I think she's plumb sorry she said all that stuff. I'd bet anything I own she'd love to have a chance to take it back. But you gotta ride down there an' let her know you're here.'

Sam's voice was flat and hard. 'I don't gotta do nothin' o' the kind. I'll size up the situation, and figure out what needs done. I'll take care of it. Then I'll get outa this country just as fast as I rode back into it.'

'Yeah, that's why we just wore out five sets o' horses an' went two nights without sleep to get here in a hurry,' Oz said with an exaggerated drawl.

Bart squirmed uncomfortably in his saddle. 'I been five nights with pert-neart no sleep,' he reminded the others. 'I'm headin' home to bed. Oz, you're welcome to hole up in our bunkhouse till Sam figures out what we're doin' next. Sam, if you're gonna be too bull-headed to go tell your woman you love her, you'd just as well hole up in the bunkhouse too.'

Oz nodded. 'Then let's go. I'm too old to run this long without sleep, an' I only rode half as far as you have.'

There was no response from Sam. The other two reined their horses around, urging them to a tired trot, leaving Sam to study the ranch yard alone. It was supper time. A thin tendril of smoke issued from the chimney. The smell of something frying in a skillet wafted on the breeze. Irritation surged at the sudden churning of his stomach the aroma aroused. Greater irritation overcame it because of the intense ache in his chest he could not stifle. It got tighter and tighter, until he felt as if he couldn't breathe. Cursing softly, he lifted his reins and turned the horse away from the yard, following the others.

His horse responded reluctantly, for a moment the weary beast had sensed the end of a long trail. As they approached the familiar yard he whinnied a response to the greeting from Billy's horse in the corral. Now he was being forced to leave that sanctuary and its promise of rest to follow the others. He was less than happy with the situation.

His emotional turmoil was nothing compared to Sam's. His stomach was constricted into a hard knot. A lump in his throat made swallowing difficult. He felt as if he bore a five hundred pound weight on his shoulders. A gaping hole ached in the center of his chest.

Everything in him screamed for him to turn back around, race for the house, throw open the door, announce his return, and pray Kate would be happy to see him. After all, Bart might be right. She just might have been as miserable as he since they separated. She might be wanting him to come back. She might . . .

He snuffed the thoughts before they could become any more unbearable. She had made her wishes perfectly clear. She didn't want to see him again. But he couldn't stay in the Indian Nation and just leave her in the peril Bart had described. He had to deal with those trying to steal her land and her security. His love would not allow him to do otherwise. When he had done so, he would leave. Only later would she learn who had rescued her. If she stewed over that, well, so be it. It was no more than she deserved, running him off her place for no reason.

14

'Whatd'ya reckon it is?'

Sam replied, 'I ain't got any idea. It's been about the same every day since I been back.'

Oz Maguire, Bart Spalding, Eduardo Spalding and Sam Heller stood in H Bar V ranch yard, studying the distant cloud of dust.

Eduardo and Bart glanced at each other, silently communicating as only brothers can. As they looked at the cloud of dust, they looked at each other, and both understood perfectly the other's assessment of the trouble it bode.

'It's gotta be pretty close to the crick,' Bart observed.

'Spring Crick?' Oz asked.

Both of the Spaldings nodded as with one mind.

'Then we'd best be checkin' it out,' Oz suggested.

'Sooner rather than later,' Sam agreed. 'We've waited too long already.'

Bart came to Sam's defense immediately. 'We really needed time to check out all of Kate's cows and horses,' he offered, 'just to make sure Russell or Grede wasn't runnin' 'em off.'

'Besides,' Eduardo added, 'you needed to have some time to think of the beautiful woman waiting there for you, whenever you get lonesome enough to not be so stubborn.'

Then he added, his eyes twinkling mischievously, 'If you were to decide such a thing, Billy would be most happy to visit at our ranch for a week or two, so the two of you could have your honeymoon.'

Sam shot a glaring look at Eduardo, but declined to answer. He said only, 'I'll get my horse saddled.'

Fifteen minutes later the quartet left the ranch yard at a swift trot. The farther they rode, the more ominous the persistent cloud of dust became. It remained in that one spot, drifting

159

slowly away on the wind, but constantly replaced by new quantities of dust arising.

An hour and a half later, Oz opined, 'It looks like it's comin' from just behind this next ridge.'

'Spring Crick runs down that valley,' Bart explained. 'It runs on to your place — uh, I mean Kate's place — about five miles down.'

Sam nodded, pretending not to notice the verbal slip. 'Let's tie our horses in that bunch of aspens, and we'll slip up on top and have a look-see.'

Moving as swiftly as silence would allow, they walked in a crouch, then crawled as they neared the crest of the hill. At its crest, each removed his hat and slipped behind rocks or scrub brush, where he could see the scene below.

That scene most closely resembled a massive mining operation, or a road-building project. The valley through which Spring Crick flowed narrowed to less than a mile at that point. Its sides steepened, forming almost vertical walls more than a hundred and fifty feet high. Both above and below the spot, the valley widened again, making this the narrowest spot in many miles of the stream's course.

Massive amounts of dirt had been and were being scraped from the surrounding prairie. Teams pulling slips scraped up, dragged, then dumped their loads of dirt in a never-ending procession. The dirt was forming a dike, more than two hundred feet wide at the bottom, that already reached more than fifty feet from the valley floor. Only in the center, where Spring Crick flowed, was the ground left at its original level. The stream still flowed unhindered, but they were clearly within a day or two of filling in that center portion as well.

'They're building a dam,' Eduardo muttered.

'They're leavin' the crick run normal, till they get the rest of it built. Then they can fill in the spot in the middle, and shut it off and make a lake.'

'A humdinger of a big one,' Oz agreed. 'If they keep buildin' clear to the top o' the valley, it'll make a dam a hundred and fifty feet deep and back up water for more'n ten miles. That's high enough to dam up that crick for two or three years before the water reaches the top.'

'Long enough to dry Kate plumb out,' Sam reasoned aloud, 'and everyone else down that crick.'

'That's what's goin' on, just as sure as blizzards are cold,' Eduardo gritted, the anger in his voice evident in his hushed tones.

Bart inserted, 'And since it's the crick and all the beaver dams and such that spreads the water out and waters the whole valley, it'll make that whole place as dry as the high plateaus. Everybody downstream will get left with no hay meadows, no winter grass, no year-round runnin' water, no nothin'.'

'So who's doin' it?' Sam asked.

Bart answered instantly, 'Russell. All

the brands I can see on the horses an' mules is his.'

'Is this land he's got a patent on?'

'Nope. He runs cows on it, but it's gov'ment range.'

'Then he doesn't have a legal right to build the dam.'

'There's no way that he could have.'

'But what are you gonna do 'bout it,' Oz pondered. 'We can't go ridin' down there an' shoot a dam.'

'There is a territorial government. You could find a lawyer and take him to court,' Bart suggested. 'The judge comes to Laramie often enough, you could get a court order to stop him.'

Eduardo snorted. 'Courts and judges are a waste of time and money. By the time the territorial courts and the fancy lawyers and politicians get done with all their word games, the valley will be without water for three years.'

'Let's ease back outa here and get back to the horses,' Sam suggested.

Accordingly, the four backed slowly away from their concealment, staying

163

below the crest of the ridge until they were well past any danger of being seen. Then they stood and walked back to the horses.

'I think we should pay a visit to the Rocking R, and put some holes in Lance Russell,' Eduardo suggested.

'That's tempting,' Sam offered qualified agreement. 'The problem is, then we'd be the ones on the wrong side of the law.'

'That's gotta be costin' an arm and a leg, hirin' all them workers and all,' Oz observed. 'Does Russell have that kinda money?'

Bart and Eduardo looked at each other, then both shrugged at the same time. Bart brought another possibility into the discussion. 'I think he's stretched himself out too thin to have that kind of cash, but Grede does. Maybe Russell's talked him into throwin' in with him.'

'Or providing the money and letting Russell take all the risk,' Eduardo offered. 'Then, since it's illegal, he can have charges filed against Russell after he has dried that woman you say you don't want out of her ranch.'

Sam stood beside his horse, leaning across his saddle, forearms resting on the seat, hands folded, lost in thought for several long minutes. He turned to the other three. 'With that many men and teams workin', how long do you reckon it'll be before they finish and shut off the water?'

The others pondered the question thoughtfully for quite a while. 'To have it completely built, a month at least,' Oz said.

'More like two, I'd guess,' Bart disagreed.

'I would say two,' Eduardo supported his brother.

'But he's only a couple days away from stoppin' the flow of the crick,' Sam said. 'I'm almost certain Grede's not involved, unless he's just loanin' Russell money. I think Oz and I'll take a little trip. When we get back, we'll see if we can shoot a little hole in a dam.'

Oz's eyebrows shot up questioningly.

Bart and Eduardo looked at each other, equally at a loss to make sense of Sam's words. Bart asked, 'How come you don't think Grede's involved?'

'I asked him,' Sam said.

That raised questions in the faces of all three of the others, but Sam declined to answer, or to appear to notice. He simply mounted his horse and rode out, heading back toward the H Bar V. The rest followed, knowing Sam would explain his plan in due time — if he had one.

15

'Who all's here?' Sam asked.

Hiram Spalding looked around the oversized front room of his sprawling ranch house. It was tightly crowded in spite of its size. Every chair was filled. Every bit of space was filled with someone sitting on the floor or leaning against the wall. Even the rest of the floor was mostly filled with men sitting cross-legged. Some chewed on match stubs, a few held steaming mugs of coffee. All eyes kept focusing on Sam, even before he spoke.

'Most of the boys from my ranch and several others,' Hiram responded. 'Half a dozen are home-steaders.'

'Rattle off all our names, then see if he can remember 'em all,' suggested Ty Henley. As he spoke, he pointed a finger at Sam. It looked like a sliver jutting from the end of an arm that neared the size of a rail-road tie.

A burst of laughter rippled around the room, relaxing the atmosphere.

'I might have a problem with that,' Sam rejoined. 'I can't remember my own name, some days.'

'Let's get down to business.' The strident voice of 'Boiling Bob' Blanchard slapped against the budding levity and squelched it instantly. 'I gotta get up and get some work done in the morning. I ain't got time to sit around jawin' all night.'

Rita Blanchard frowned and spoke softly into her husband's ear. He fell silent, but his face reflected a roiling impatience, nonetheless.

'I 'spect we'd just as well get to what I asked you all here for,' Hiram conceded. 'We seem to have us a problem with Russell's outfit wantin' to take over and run the rest of us out of the country.'

'You're big enough he ain't gonna run over you,' the soft voice of Lafe Sorenson replied.

'Not for now, anyway,' Hiram acknowledged. 'But that ain't true for any of the rest of you. And if he picks your outfits off, one at a time, he'll be big enough to take me on as well. Besides, I'm too much of a neighbor to just sit by and watch it happen to any of you.'

'What's Russell doin' up there on Spring Crick?' another homesteader asked. 'I see a cloud o' dust up there pertneart every day for over a month. He bustin' sod or somethin'?'

It was Sam who responded. 'He's building a big dam across the whole draw, to dam up Spring Crick.'

Deathly silence fell across the room. Ty Henley spoke first. 'That'd put me outa business. I'm on Spring Crick, just a couple miles down from the Bond place.'

'Me too, about six miles farther down,' another homesteader joined in. 'Without that crick, I got no live water on my place.'

'Ain't that on government range?' another probed.

169

Sam nodded. 'Yeah, it's government range. Russell runs cattle on it, but he's got no title to it.'

'Then how can he put a dam there?'

' 'Cause he can, and who's gonna stop him?'

'Somebody better put a stop to it.'

'There's enough of us, we could ride over there and offer to let him stop what he's doin', or get tarred and feathered and rode outa the country on a rail.'

'He's got a bunch of gun hands hired. We might outnumber 'em, but I ain't sure we'd win against 'em.'

'We could try.'

'That'd cause a range war, sure's anything.'

'But if we don't do somethin', he can do the same thing with Clear Crick and Cottonwood Crick, and then we're all outa business.'

The conversations ran around in circles for several minutes, offering no solutions, but pretty clearly defining the issues and problems. When it had gone on long enough, Sam spoke up.

'I can deal with the dam. Oz, Bart, Eddie, and I will do that. But what happens afterward is where we need to be united.'

'How you gonna deal with a dam?' Boiling Bob interrupted, his voice dripping with skepticism. 'You can't go over there and start shoveling. I seen that thing they're buildin'. It'd be like movin' a mountain to get it outa there.'

'I'll take care of that part,' Sam assured him. 'But when I do, Russell's gonna come bustin' over here with every gun he's got. If we stick together, we can take care of him and his gunslingers all at one time. If we don't, he'll run us all outa the country, one at a time.'

'Or kill us all, one at a time,' Lafe Sorenson said softly. Then he added, 'Just like he did Ralph Bond. And Tennessee Sneed. And Dick Coggins.'

'And Al Tenner,' another voice added.

Silence fell across the room, as the

assembled group remembered those of their neighbors who had met sudden and suspicious deaths.

'So we obviously gotta do somethin',' Ty Henley summarized the collective mindset. 'I guess it's up to you to tell us what.'

Sam nodded. 'The night of the fifteenth — that's almost two weeks away — I'll sorta make the dam disappear. By sunup, I'm bettin' Russell and his whole outfit'll head straight for Kate Bond's place, hell-for-leather. If all of you are already set up a ways ahead of there, well hidden until my signal, and all in the right place, we can have his whole outfit surrounded and out-gunned. When they see the setup, they'll give it up. Hopefully we can do it without havin' to fire a shot.'

'You're dreamin',' Boiling Bob retorted. 'Them's professional gunfighters.'

'That's exactly why Sam's right,' Lafe Sorenson responded instantly. 'If they were all hotheaded cowboys, they might try to shoot their way out. Professional gunfighters know better than to buck the odds when the deck's stacked too heavy against 'em. They'll back down quick.'

A few seconds of silence followed, then voices exploded from all corners of the room, some enthusiastically in favor of the plan, some hesitantly so, some flatly opposed.

'Why don't we just let the law handle it?' Sonia Sorenson asked.

Her question silenced the room until her own husband responded. 'The only thing the law could do is either raise a posse and face Russell head-on, on his own ground, or call in the army. Facing him on his own ground would be an all-out gun battle, and a lot of people would get killed. Calling in the army would take months to get authorized, as long as nobody's under siege or anything. By then, I'll be dried out, along with all of you that live on Spring Crick, and Russell will already be workin' on the next crick.'

Another long silence ensued. It was,

again, Lafe Sorenson who said, 'When do you want us at your place?'

His wife, Sonia, visibly gasped when he said it. She stared at him as if she had just been, somehow, betrayed, but she said nothing. She pressed her lips into a thin line and stared at the floor. Lafe did his best to ignore her reaction.

'He ain't gonna ignore that when he gets home,' Sam thought.

Aloud he said, 'We'll need everybody's help a few nights before. Then the night we take care of the dam, we'll get set up before daylight where the road goes through that cut about a mile south of the Bond place. Even if they decide to hit here, or one of the other places first, they'll almost sure come that way.'

'Are you gonna be there?'

'I'll be there,' Sam promised, 'before any of the festivities begin.'

Silent nods from most of the men present signified their commitment. Sam didn't know these men, but he knew a hundred like them, spread across the rough and ready west. He knew that nod of agreement was more dependable and binding than any piece of paper sworn in a court of law.

That the matter was settled was indicated almost immediately, when one of Spalding's hands said, 'Hey, Ty! Let's see you arm wrestle Bart.'

A dozen voices immediately offered enthusiastic support for the idea. As if he had been awaiting the moment, Eduardo carried a small table in and set it in the middle of the room. It was no sooner in place than two chairs were placed across from each other.

Bart looked at Ty. Ty shrugged and rose to his feet. He was every bit as tall as Bart, and boasted shoulders at least as broad. His hands appeared bigger than Bart's, but other than that the two appeared evenly matched.

At once quiet bets were placed between friends all around the room. Bart and Ty sat down facing each other and placed their elbows on the table. When they had their hands gripped together in a way that suited both, they nodded. Hiram stood with his hand atop theirs for a moment, then jerked his hand away. 'Go!' he said.

Instantly each man strained against the grip of the other, hoping a slightly quicker reaction time would provide a quick win. It worked for neither. For each, it was like trying to push the trunk of a tree over. Muscles bulged. Faces reddened. Ty's shirt sleeve ripped abruptly, unable to stretch far enough to house the giant muscle within it. The eyes of both men bulged with the effort. Jaw muscles bunched as teeth gritted. They strained against each other in silence, exerting every ounce of their immense strength. Their knotted fists failed to move in either direction.

Every eye in the room was riveted on those two knotted fists. Unseen, Camilla Spalding slipped up behind Bart. She suddenly poked him with an index finger in both ribs, and yelled, 'Boo!'

Bart yelled as if he'd been struck by a rattlesnake. He leaped from the chair, sending it flying backward. It narrowly missed Camilla as she swiftly side-stepped, knowing exactly the reaction her brother would have.

Bart turned menacingly toward his little sister. She saucily stuck her tongue out at him, then turned and ran.

A delayed roar of laughter erupted as the assembled group realized what had happened. Hiram shook his head ruefully. He addressed his wife. 'Eva, would you do something with that daughter of yours?'

'My daughter?' Eva retorted. 'She gets that from your side of the family, not from mine.'

The retort stirred a second round of laughter. One man's call for the two to resume their contest went unanswered and unheeded. The moment of levity passed and all bets were considered canceled. Each one remembered the reason for their being there. Conversations were muted and few as they all filed from the room and mounted their horses for the ride home.

16

'These mules are sure slow.'

Sam smiled tightly. The strain he felt was betrayed by the rigidity of his shoulders, the set of his jaw. 'That's why I'm usin' 'em,' he responded.

'A wagon would've worked just as well.'

'Do you want to ride in a wagon with that much dynamite?'

Oz shrugged. 'We could've padded it with a lot of straw.'

'We could've,' Sam agreed. 'I'd rather trust the mules. They're awful sure-footed.'

'They are that,' Oz agreed. It was obvious his agreement was reluctant. 'If I was movin' that slow, I'd be sure-footed too.'

Six mules wended their way along the side of the hill. They were strung together with a single line, so they moved single-file. Five of the six were each loaded with four cases of dynamite. They were lashed into place with carefully knotted diamond hitches, that either Sam or Oz checked every hour or so. The sixth mule had a different pack, containing enormous coils of black wick and caps.

'Are you sure you can get this all to go off at the same time?' Oz asked for at least the dozenth time.

Sam smiled again, through the dust and dirt that coated them both. 'It'll go,' he assured his friend.

'Where'd you learn to use this stuff anyway?'

'I worked in a mine for a month once.'

'Just a month?'

'That was enough.'

'Didn't like dynamite that much, huh?'

'Didn't mind the dynamite. I did mind bein' underground. I promised the guy I'd help him for a month. I swore to God if I survived that month

I'd never go underground again till I do it face up, with somebody pattin' me in the face with a shovel.'

'If one o' them mules stumbles, that may be before you think.'

Sam smiled more broadly. 'If one of those mules stumbles, neither one of us will need burying.'

'Whatd'ya mean?'

'I mean what's left of us will be scattered far enough nobody's gonna gather up the pieces anyway.'

'I always sorta wanted to go out layin' in a soft bed with my hands folded nice an' peaceful across my chest.'

'You want a flower in your hands too?'

'A half pint o' whiskey'd be better.'

'Why? You couldn't drink it then.'

'Yeah, but it'd be nice to know I had it along, just in case.'

'I always thought I'd rather have a box o' bakin' soda.'

Oz looked at his friend quizzically. 'Bakin' soda? What for?'

'Bakin' soda works pretty good for puttin' out fires. I thought maybe a box of it might at least give me a little space.'

Oz snorted, then chuckled. 'Maybe you'd best have your whole casket filled with it, then.'

'Good idea. That'll be your job, to make sure that's done.'

'The Indians do that.'

'What, use bakin' soda?'

'No, not that. But they bury their dead with what they figger they might need in the next life. They bury 'em with a bow and arrows, or whatever. I heard of one, once, that they buried with his horse.'

'If you get to take with you whatever's buried with you, I'd rather have a woman.'

'Someplace in Asia or somewhere they do that, too. They build a great big fire to burn up the dead guy's body. His widow's supposed to throw herself into the fire and burn up with him.'

'What if she don't wanta do that?'

'Then somebody has to kill her and throw her into the fire. That way they figure he'll have her for a wife in the next life.'

'Really? I wonder if it works.'

'Don't guess anyone's come back to let 'em know. I doubt it. It'd save havin' to provide for the widow, though.'

'I wonder if she'd think it was heaven, if she was still stuck with the same man.'

'Not if he looked like you, she wouldn't.'

'I sorta noticed that you're still batchin' too.'

Oz abruptly brought the conversation back from its escapist banter. 'What are we gonna do when we get there?'

Sam's instant reply indicated the thought he had already given to the matter. 'There's a thick bunch of timber just over the ridge from where they're buildin' the dam. I figured we could hide the stuff there, then get the rest of the boys to come help.'

'You gonna do it all in one night?'

'Nope. I wanta get everything in place in one night. Then we'll cover up our tracks, and wait till the right time.'

'How you gonna keep 'em from noticin'?'

'I'll show you. I think I got it figured out.'

They rode mostly in silence the rest of the day. They talked little when they turned into their bedrolls for the night, and were up before daylight. They loaded the increasingly reluctant mules, grateful it would be the last day on the trail.

The sun was just dipping beyond the western mountains when they stopped in a finger of heavy timber. Although they knew they were just across the ridge from the growing earthen dam, they heard no activity. 'You don't s'pose they're done, do you?'

'I doubt it. Just knocked off for the day, I'd guess.'

'Let's have a look-see.'

Together they worked their way to the top of the ridge and looked over.

The dam stretched clear across the narrow valley, more than thirty feet high in the center. The center had been filled in, so that the stream's flow of water was halted. Sam's jaw muscles bulged with the clenching of his teeth. Fire flashed from his eyes as he stared at the dry streambed below the dam.

Silently the pair descended the slope to the timber. 'They're still workin' to make it higher,' Oz observed. 'The slips and stuff are all still there.'

Sam nodded. Gruffly he said, 'Let's get this stuff taken care of.'

They spread a tarpaulin on a flat spot of ground and stacked the cases of explosives on it. They covered it with tarpaulins and tied them securely enough to ensure even a violent thunderstorm would not allow them to get wet.

When they finished, they mounted their horses. Sam picked up the lead line for the mules. 'Let's get some shut-eye. We'll see if we can have as many guys as possible here at sundown tomorrow.'

184

Silently they rode away into the gathering darkness. Sam wavered minute by minute between conflicting emotions: anger at the dam and its effects boiled within him; weariness nagged at his body; relief flooded through him that they had the dynamite transported safely. Excitement at the prospect of what lay ahead made him tingle with anticipation. Eclipsing all of it was thoughts of Kate, still not knowing he was back in the country. He ached to go to her, but his pride held him firmly in check.

He'd ride back to the H Bar V bunkhouse where he was staying and tomorrow he'd continue with the plan — he'd take care of Kate's problems; he'd make sure she and Billy were secure and free from parasites seeking to steal her land and cattle. Then he'd ride back to the Indian Nation where he belonged.

The thought surged in the back of his mind that he should at least give her an opportunity to take back the things she had said. He fought the idea down instantly. That would be too much like begging, and he wouldn't beg for the love of any woman. She had made herself perfectly clear — she never wanted to see him again. She ordered him off her place. That was that. His love for her wouldn't allow him to leave her in jeopardy, but she would have her wish. She would never see him again.

17

'It looks like the whole country turned out.'

Sam looked around the large hollow. They were just over the ridge from the huge dam Russell's men were building. The sun had just sunk below the mountains to the west, casting their long shadows across the land like harbingers of doom. The impression was reflected in the faces of nearly all those assembled.

It appeared that every small rancher and homesteader in the country had arrived. There were more than a hundred people assembled, including many of the wives and older children. Every person held the shovel they had been asked to bring.

Oz joined the group, striding down from the top of the ridge where he had been ensconced in a clump of brush.

'Everybody gone?' Sam asked.

Oz nodded. 'Long gone an' clear outa sight.'

'Then let's get started,' Sam said.

He turned to the assembled crowd. 'I can't thank all of you enough for being here tonight. With this many people, we can get the job done in great shape. The dam Russell's building is just over the top of that ridge,' he explained, in case some of them didn't know. 'We need to dig a ditch all the way across it, about twenty-five foot down from the top of where it's built up to. We need to dig it as deep as we can in the time we have, leavin' time to fill it up again before we leave.'

Some of those assembled sported slowly spreading grins as they intuited Sam's plan. One of them, whose name Sam didn't know, put it into words. 'You gonna lay dynamite in the ditch, then?'

Heads snapped up in sudden understanding. Every eye focused on Sam, awaiting his reply.

Sam nodded, smiling. 'That's exactly what we're gonna do. Then we'll bury it, with everything set and ready, and the wicks run over the ridge to here. Then all we have to do when it's time is light it off.'

One of the wives spoke up. 'Won't they notice where we've dug the ditch?'

Sam shook his head. 'It's all fresh dirt. If we smooth the ground out over the ditch again, they'll just keep adding dirt on top and burying it deeper.'

'That'd take a mighty big pile o' dynamite to string out that far,' somebody objected.

'We've got plenty. We decided we might not have enough the first trip, so Oz and I made another trip to Laramie and doubled up on what we'd bought. Over there underneath those tarps is enough dynamite to do the job in good shape.'

'Then we'd best get started,' another voice suggested. 'The moon's already comin' up.'

With no further talk, the group

trooped up the hill and over the ridge. They spread out in a line that reached clear across the raw earth of the new dam. Sam indicated where he wanted the ditch, and shovels began throwing dirt with a swift rhythm.

A crooked ditch swiftly took form across the span of earth. Uphill from the ditch, Sam, Oz, Bart, and Eduardo rolled out four reels of black-wick. They stretched them over the top of the ridge, ending the first one at the nearest end of the dam, and ending the other three so that their ends were evenly spaced the length of the ditch. The last one reached within fifty feet of the far end.

'How you gonna get 'em all to go off at the same time?' Oz eventually asked. 'They're all different lengths.'

Sam nodded. 'The first one'll be the only one to go off, if it works right.'

The other three stopped what they were doing and stared at him, obviously confused.

He explained. 'Dynamite don't blow

up from a spark. I've watched guys unwrap a stick of dynamite, then stick a cigarette in it. The cigarette just went out.'

'Then what makes it blow up?'

'Concussion. Shock. It's actually sawdust that's soaked in nitroglycerine. The wick, that's stuck into the middle of a stick of dynamite, makes the cap blow up. The cap blowin' up is what sets off the dynamite. We'll lay out the dynamite so every stick overlaps the one ahead of it. The jar of one stick blowin' up will set off the next one, and the next and the next and so on all the way across the canyon. It'll happen so fast it'll be like they all went up at the same time. Once the first stick blows up, the rest'll happen without waitin' for the other wicks to burn to the cap.'

'Then how come we're puttin' these others in?'

'Just in case things don't work quite right. If there ends up bein' too much space between sticks, it might stop things. Then the next wick will start it up again.'

'So one of 'em is enough to do the job, and the rest are just insurance?'

'Exactly.'

The three thought about it for a few seconds. Bart finally said, 'I'd have never thought of that. Good to have insurance.'

When the ditch was as deep as he wanted, Sam called off the crew. They gathered, wiping sweat from their faces, awaiting further orders.

'Now we need to get the dynamite into the ditches,' he announced. 'Oz will show you where it is. Any of you that don't mind handlin' dynamite grab a handful and bring it to me, or lay it out along the high side of the ditch. We'll start from one end and lay it out in the bottom of the ditch. But let me remind you of something, in case any of you haven't handled dynamite — dynamite don't blow up from a spark or fire. It blows up from a jar. That means don't drop it. Don't try to carry more than you can carry without dropping any. It ain't likely that just droppin' a stick would make it go, but I don't want to take any chances. As you bring it to us, we'll get it laid out in the ditch. As soon as we've got it laid out a ways, some of you can come along behind and fill the ditch up over the top of it. If you've got a big rock, don't throw it into the ditch until there's plenty of dirt on top of the dynamite. That could set it off too.'

He felt as if he had just made a long speech like a politician, but he needed to be sure they understood what to do. He waited to see if anyone had questions, but most had already started for the other side of the ridge where the dynamite waited.

By the time the first of them arrived with armfuls of the explosive, Sam had inserted the end of the shortest black-wick into a cap, crimping it tightly with his teeth. He opened the end of a stick of dynamite and inserted the cap into its center, rolling the paper carefully around it again. He laid it in the bottom of the ditch and positioned three more sticks directly on top of it. Then he and Oz began laying out dynamite in two overlapping rows in the bottom of the ditch. They were placed end to end in the two rows, so the ends of those in one row were exactly in the center of those in the row lying against its side.

Following his instructions, as he and Oz laid out the dynamite, Bart and Eduardo followed. They shoved dirt down on to the dynamite, packing it by hand around the explosive to cover it and keep it in place.

It was quickly apparent that they weren't going to use half the dynamite he and Oz had secured. They began to lay three rows of the reddish brown cylinders instead of two, then increased it to four. Through the center of the dam they increased it to five rows.

By the time they had proceeded fifty feet, others began filling in the ditch, smoothing it over, erasing all signs of its presence.

They finished fully two hours earlier than Sam had hoped. By the soft light of the full moon, he walked the length of the nearly finished dam. He looked at the moon's reflection on the considerable lake already pent up behind it. He hoped it wasn't deep enough yet to cause problems from the wall of water that would surge down the valley when the dam was breached.

As he thought of that surge of water, he mentally measured the distance of the creek from Kate's house. He studied, in his mind's eye, the lift of ground from creek to house, measuring how many feet of water would be necessary to threaten the house and yard. He studied the backed up water in the newly formed reservoir again. He knew Kate and Billy should be in no danger, but his stomach was knotted in fear nonetheless.

He pulled the kerchief from his back pocket to wipe away the sweat from his face. As he did, he smelled again the fragrant piece of soft soap he still kept carefully saved within it.

He had nearly run out of the soap Kate had placed amongst his things when he had abruptly and angrily left. When he was down to that one last sliver of the fragrant substance, he could not bring himself to use it. He kept it carefully wrapped in his kerchief, smelling it whenever he wiped sweat or dirt from his face. Every time, as now, it wakened the ache in his gut as if a mule had kicked him.

He stuffed the kerchief back into his pocket angrily, vowing again to get rid of that last reminder of what would never be. Even as he did, he knew deep down he wouldn't ever be able to do so. He'd keep it there, and let it keep tearing his heart apart every time he smelled it, until it eventually lost its fragrance.

He strode to the end of the dam, where his tired crew waited. 'Let's erase as many signs of our presence as we can and get out of here,' he said, his voice gruffer than he intended.

Nobody seemed to notice the abrupt harshness of his tone.

It was Bart that put the nagging worry in the back of his mind into words. 'There's gonna be a pretty big bunch o' water barrelin' down that valley when the dam blows,' he observed. 'You don't reckon it'll flood Kate out do you?'

Sam shook his head. 'It shouldn't. The house is quite a bit higher than the crick. It wouldn't hurt to let her know about it, though, just in case.'

Eduardo eyed Sam appraisingly. 'It would be the good thing for you to ride there and tell her what is about to happen.'

Sam glared at him in sudden anger, but held his tongue. When he had better control, he said, 'You can let her know. She don't want me on her place.'

'I think she is wishing more than anything to have you on her place,' Eduardo argued softly.

'Now what would make you think that?'

'My mother has visited her two or three times since you have come back. She says that Kate is a very miserable woman without you, and very much wants for you to come and say that you are sorry, so she can say so too.'

'I got nothin' to apologize for,' Sam retorted. 'She's the one that kicked me off her place. If she's got something to say, she's the one that needs to come and say it. If your Ma's been over there blabbin', then she knows where I am.'

Eduardo nodded. 'She knows. My mother has tried to tell her to ride over and talk to you, but it seems that she is just as stubborn as you are, my friend. She says it is you who must make the first move.'

Sam acted as if he were going to respond, then wheeled and stalked away instead. He busied himself with making sure the black-wicks were well hidden where they snaked over the top of the ridge. Using one of the tarpaulins that had covered the dynamite and wicks, he ensured that the ends of the wicks would stay perfectly dry until time for them to be lighted.

The first streaks of dawn were reaching fingers into the eastern sky as the four of them rode away, following the trail of the tired crew of workers that had dispersed as soon as the last of the dynamite was buried.

18

After supper on a ranch is usually a time to sit around, swap tall tales, roll a couple of cigarettes and relax. This night on the H Bar V there was none of that casual atmosphere in evidence. It was replaced by a silent and tense air of expectation.

Most of the hands had already retired to the bunkhouse. Sam knew they would all turn in early, then lay sleepless in their bunks until the middle of the night. Then they would all saddle up and ride to what might well be the last place they would see in this world.

He, Oz, Bart, and Eduardo were already saddled. They were just getting ready to step into saddles, when the dogs announced the approach of a rider.

All four instinctively moved around

behind their horses as they waited to see who would be arriving at this late hour.

The fading light caught a glint of reflection from a star on the rider's vest as he trotted into the yard.

Hiram Spalding stepped out of the house to greet him. 'Howdy Harm,' he called out. 'Ridin' a little late in the day, ain't you? You missed supper, but git down and come in. We'll rustle up a bait o' grub for you.'

Harm Denton stopped his horse half a dozen paces in front of the rancher. He stepped from the saddle. 'Howdy, Hi,' he responded.

Instead of answering the rancher's invitation, he addressed the other four. 'You boys look like you're headin' out kinda late.'

The four looked at each other uncertainly. As one, they turned their gazes back to Hiram, clearly seeking a cue from him about how much to entrust to the marshal.

Hiram showed no hesitation. 'Busy

night comin',' he confirmed the marshal's observation. 'Glad you just happened to show up.'

'What're you boys up to?'

'Have you heard about the dam Russell's built on Spring Crick?'

The marshal's head jerked up. 'Dam? On Spring Crick? That don't even run through Russell's place, does it?'

'It runs through land he grazes, but you're right. It's government land. You know that spot where it goes through that red rock canyon?'

The marshal nodded. 'I know the spot.'

'He's built a dam clear across the canyon there.'

The marshal stared at the rancher in disbelief. 'Why, a dam across there would stop up Spring Crick for miles and miles. That'd put every outfit downstream from there plumb outa business.'

'Not to mention it's illegal, since it's on government range.'

'You gonna get an injunction?'

'Too late. He's already got the crick stopped up.'

'So what are you boys aimin' to do about it?'

Sam decided it might be best for him to offer the answer. 'We thought maybe we'd ride over there and move that dam outa the canyon.'

The marshal stared incomprehendingly. 'How in the world do you think you're gonna do that?'

'Three nights ago we laid enough dynamite in the middle of that dam to do the job. All we gotta do tonight is light it off.'

The marshal stared for a long moment, digesting the information.

'I ain't sure that's entirely legal,' he said finally.

'Why not,' Hiram challenged. 'We're just removin' somethin' from government range that had no legal right to be there in the first place. It's no crime if we aren't damagin' anyone else's property. It ain't Russell's property, 'cause it ain't on his land.'

The marshal frowned a long moment, then slowly a grin spread out beneath his large mustache. 'I'd have to say you're plumb right. Mind if I ride along?'

'Proud to have you,' Sam responded at once.

'That ain't what brought you here, though,' Hiram guessed.

'Well, no, it ain't. Actually, I rode over here to ask for a bit of help. I was hopin' some of your boys would be willin' to form up a posse to give me a hand servin' a warrant.'

'What kind of warrant?'

'I found out there's an old warrant on Russell from down in New Orleans. It seems he sorta disappeared with all the bankroll of a gamblin' outfit an' whore-house that him and another fella was partners in. He killed the other fella in the process, so there's a warrant out for him, for both robbery and murder.'

Silence settled over the group like a gossamer shroud for a full minute, as each digested the information, and its ramifications.

Sam put their thinking into words. 'When we blow that dam, Russell will plumb certain come ridin' hell-for-leather with that whole gang o' gun hands he's got hired. He'll be real anxious to wipe out the ones he'll figure are responsible. We're almost as certain what way he'll come. We got it set up to be ready for 'em, and hopefully convince 'em to give up without a fight. That'd be the perfect time to arrest him.'

The marshal considered it for a long moment. Finally he said, 'And you got this whole party set up for tonight, I take it?'

'Yup.'

'Done sent out the invitations, decorated the barn, an' hired the fiddler, huh?'

Sam grinned. 'We sorta left the barn out of it. Hiram's kinda tetchy about his barn.'

'Well, if I was to deputize this bunch

you got ready, I reckon that'd make it an official act of the government to restore government range to its rightful condition, and bring to justice certain nefarious criminal elements of the territory.'

Eduardo mirrored Sam's grin. 'Now that is what I call feeling the sunshine of the saints smiling upon us. It is a sign, my friends. This night will be wondrous.'

'Not to mention a heap o' fun,' Bart echoed.

'Don't go gettin' to cocky,' Sam cautioned. 'Russell and his men ain't likely to roll over without a fight.'

The cold reality of his words instantly chilled the growing sense of enthusiasm. Even so, it was better than any of them could possibly have hoped. As the five rode out together, Sam couldn't keep his own spirits from soaring.

19

'They left most of the slips sittin' right on top of the dam,' Bart whispered.

'You probably don't need to whisper,' Sam responded. 'They're all back at Russell's by this time of night.'

'Do you think he will even know what we have done before they come tomorrow to work some more?'

Sam grinned. 'Oh, I 'spect they'll know. Russell's ranch is only a couple miles away. I do 'spect they'll notice all right.'

'So let's get it done,' Oz fretted.

Sam carefully removed the tarpaulin covering from the ends of the black-wicks. He drew his knife and cut a foot off the end of each.

'What're you doin' that for?' Oz querried.

'Makin' sure I'm down to fresh powder,' Sam explained.

He thought for a minute, then said, 'Instead of me lightin' these one at a time, why don't you each grab a fuse and get a match. We can light 'em together that way.'

'That should give us plenty time to get to the top of the hill where we can watch,' Eduardo opined.

Sam frowned. 'We for sure ain't gonna do that.'

The others looked at him with obvious surprise, mingled with disappointment. He realized suddenly they had all expected to watch the explosion.

'When that thing goes, there's gonna be rocks an' dirt comin' down like rain in a frog-drowner. We're gonna be down there in the trees, hangin' on to our horses for all we're worth, not standin' up on top like we're watchin' a circus.'

The wisdom of his words slowly crowded out their hopes of seeing the results of their work, and one by one they nodded their agreement.

Sam handed each of his three friends

the end of a black-wick. Each fished a match from a vest pocket. When he saw they were ready, he said, 'Let's do it.'

He and Oz lifted a leg and swiped the match across the tightly stretched fabric of their pants, igniting their matches. Bart and Eduardo flicked the head of their matches with a thumb nail, evoking an equal response. Four matches flared beneath the ends of four lengths of black-wick, carefully cupped in hands that shielded the small flames from the breeze. Four wicks sputtered to life, the fire at their ends rapidly climbing through the grass toward the crest of the ridge.

As one, the five men grabbed the reins of their horses and raced for the bottom of the large basin, and the protection of the thick stand of trees. Well within the trees, each looped the reins of his horse around a tree, knotted them securely, then added the security of firmly grasping the jaw-strap of his horse's bridle.

They waited, scarcely daring to

breathe. A minute passed, then two. They began to look at each other, wondering why nothing was happening. Another minute passed, then another. Four men stared hard at Sam, trying to read his expression. Sam stared straight ahead, ignoring them.

A fifth minute passed. Sam tensed and tightened his grip on his horse's bridle. Seeing his slight action, the others did the same.

A muffled thump from the other side of the ridge threatened to overwhelm the waiting five, but they didn't have time to even feel its threat. At the heels of that thump, a growing rumble erupted into the sky. It escalated to the loudest sound any of them had ever heard. It physically hurt their ears, shaking the ground beneath their feet. Horses' ears flattened back against lifted heads. Nostrils flared. Five horses fought frantically to tear loose and flee.

A noise louder than any of them could ever have imagined roared upward from the earth, spewing dirt, rocks, abandoned equipment, and gravel half a mile into the air. The ground shook and trembled as if it would open up beneath them and swallow them whole.

'Duck your heads,' Sam yelled, stretching himself over the head of his panicked horse to shield its head as best he could.

The others did the same, but even so were stunned by the volume of dirt and rocks that rained down on them. It ripped branches from trees. It filled the air with dust and dirt, choking off their supply of air. They were all filled with the instant panic of being buried alive.

Then it was over. Dust swirled in the air, carried away by the night breeze. Four men swept off their hats, swatting the dirt from them against their legs, coughing the dirt from their airways.

'Bart's down,' Oz noticed first.

The others instantly ran to him. Just as they reached him, he started to moan. 'You OK, brother?' Eduardo demanded.

Bart did not answer. He sat up slowly. His eyes slowly focused. He blinked rapidly. 'What happened?' he mumbled, scarcely intelligibly.

He struggled to his feet, slowly regaining his equilibrium. 'I think you tried to see if your head was as hard as one of the rocks that was falling,' Eduardo suggested. 'If I am to guess, I think the rock is probably shattered into small gravel.'

'Good to know it didn't hit any part of him that he ever uses,' Sam chimed in.

The rest vented their relief with similar barbs and jabs until Bart seemed to have recovered. Straightening his smashed hat, he placed it gingerly on his head. 'Good thing I wasn't bad hurt,' he groused. 'I could've laid here till spring waitin' to get any sympathy from this outfit.'

'Let's go see what we did,' Sam interrupted.

Suddenly remembering the purpose of their being there, the five trooped together up the hill. The ground was covered with several inches of dirt and rocks. The loose footing made the climb slow and laborious, but they reached the top together.

The waning of the full moon was more than adequate to illuminate the land. Nothing whatever remained of the accursed dam. For as far as they could see down the canyon, the ground was covered with two or three feet of dirt and debris. In the center, the newly formed reservoir had become a rushing, muddy torrent, pouring down the canyon, carrying with it the remaining dirt that had stemmed its flow.

'You 'spect you used enough dynamite?' the marshal asked.

'Looks pretty good to me,' Oz answered for his friend.

'That's a lot o' water headin' downstream,' Bart fretted. 'Don't you reckon you'd oughta hightail it down to Kate's place, to make sure they're OK?'

Sam shot him a glance that said,

'Nice try!' but he didn't bother to answer.

Instead Eduardo surprisingly shot down his brother's effort. 'It will spread out and slow down when it hits the flats,' he reasoned. 'From there it will run more slowly. It will not rise high enough to reach the house.'

Bart glared incredulously at his brother for a long moment. Finally he said, 'Fine lot o' help you are!'

Sam had neither the patience nor desire for their banter. 'We'd best be headin' back to get set up. You can bet Russell's already got somebody headin' over here on a dead run to find out what happened.'

They retreated to the battered copse where their horses still stirred nervously. Each of them examined his horse carefully, noting each bruise and bump, making sure their animals were not seriously injured from the falling dirt and rocks.

They mounted up and rode out, their horses' hoof beats muffled by the thick dirt and dust that covered the earth. They rode for a good half mile before they got beyond it.

'I sure wish you would've used a bit more dynamite,' the marshal observed with a straight face. 'We coulda spread that fine fresh dirt clear across Wyoming, instead o' just half way.'

Sam was too preoccupied to bother answering.

20

'Everybody all set?'

The question was superfluous, but Sam answered the marshal anyway. 'Yup.'

'Already they're coming,' Eduardo called out softly.

Sam couldn't hear a thing, but he already knew better than to challenge the elder of the Spalding boy's hearing. 'Everybody get set,' he called out in response.

Out of sight along both sides of the road he heard rifles chambering rounds. Hammers clicked back to full cock. Boot soles scraped against rocks. Clothes and leather rustled in the semi-darkness of early dawn. Then all fell silent.

Sam heard it then. The distant thunder of three dozen horses, coming fast.

'Sure enough in a hurry,' the marshal muttered beside him.

'What'dya bet we slow 'em down some,' Sam responded.

In the growing light, the galloping company hove into view around a bend of the road. When they were directly between the two hidden halves of the welcoming committee they were unaware of, Sam and the marshal stepped suddenly out from behind the boulder each had waited behind.

The marshal barked, 'Stop right where you are!'

The startled group hauled back on their reins, skidding their horses to a surprised halt.

'Throw up your hands!' the marshal ordered. 'I have a warrant for Lance Russell's arrest, and I mean to have all your guns.'

Russell spit out his response in a burst of profanity. The marshal ignored it. 'You men are surrounded. Throw down your guns.'

In response, men stood on the banks

that rose along both sides of the road, showing themselves.

Instead of surrender, Russell's band of gunmen dove from their saddles, as if at some prearranged signal. They hit the ground firing at those above them, and diving for cover behind rocks and brush.

Russell and the man riding beside him wheeled their horses and jammed spurs into their sides, leaning forward tightly on to the pommels of their saddles, making themselves as small a target as possible.

Bullets rained down around them, but it was impossible to tell if either was hit. The men on the ground were not so fortunate — in minutes, every man among them was dead or wounded. Those able to do so threw aside their weapons and raised their hands.

At the first response of Russell, Sam and the marshal had ducked back behind rocks, from where they directed a withering fire from ground level. The marshal was unscathed.

Oz was not so fortunate. He fell victim to one of the first shots fired from the gunmen. No sooner had the surviving members surrendered than Bart called out, 'Sam! Oz is down.'

Sam sprinted to his friend, panic rising in his throat. His first glance confirmed his worst fears. Oz's breath came in short gasps. A bright froth ringed his mouth. He reached up a hand to grasp the one Sam reached out with. He started to say something, but had no breath to make it audible. It died in his throat as his body relaxed. His head lolled to one side, eyes staring at nothing.

Tenderly Sam reached out and closed his friend's eyes. Oz's words whispered in his mind. 'I always sorta wanted to go out layin' in a soft bed with my hands folded nice an' peaceful across my chest.'

'Didn't even get his last wish,' he muttered, fighting the waves of grief surging up within him.

As he stood, Bart said, 'You're hit too.'

Sam nodded. 'No big deal. Clipped my arm. I'm goin' after Russell.'

'I will ride with you,' a voice at his shoulder declared.

Sam turned, surprised to find the statement had come from Lafe Sorenson. 'Two of us will ride faster and not be as obvious when we get there,' he said.

His tone of voice sounded totally foreign to the lanky homesteader Sam had come to know. It also conveyed an unmistakable message that it was he, not Sam, that was now in charge.

Sam simply nodded and retrieved his horse. 'Bart and I will ride with you,' Eduardo announced.

Sam shook his head. 'The marshal will need you boys' help with the prisoners and the wounded. We'll take care of Russell.'

It was little more than an hour later that the pair rode slowly into the yard of Russell's ranch. It seemed eerily deserted. Not even the usual dogs had come to greet their arrival. Their eyes darted around the yard, probing every possible hiding spot for the ambush they would have bet waited for them.

They stepped off their horses. Sam noted with concern how stiff his right arm had already become. His shirt and jacket sleeve were soaked with blood. The blood had run down on to his hand, making it, he realized suddenly, too slick to grip his gun firmly and surely.

Just then Lance Russell and another man stepped out from behind a shed. Sam barely heard the slight grunt of recognition from Sorenson as he and the homesteader turned to face the duo.

'You ain't got no smarts at all, Heller,' Russell announced, 'comin' here without your army.'

Ignoring him, the man at his right addressed Sorenson. 'Didn't expect to find you here, Frank.'

'Long way from Laredo, Clint,'

Sorenson responded.

'I always did wonder if I could beat you,' the gunman responded.

Puzzled, but refusing to be distracted, Sam addressed Russell. 'The marshal has a warrant for you from New Orleans,' he announced. 'I aim to arrest you or leave you dead.'

'Do you think just two of you can do that?' Lance challenged.

'It's over, Russell,' Sam countered. 'You boys drop your guns.'

As if that were the signal they awaited, both Russell and the man Sorenson had called Clint whipped their guns from their holsters.

Sam recognized the signal in Russell's eyes, even before he saw his hand move. His hand was already gripping his own pistol. As he lifted it, he felt his blood-soaked hand slip on the grip. He tightened his hold, knowing even as he did that the extra effort would slow him down far too much. Both of the men he faced were far, far too fast for him to survive that much delay in his own draw.

At his left, Sorenson's gun roared just as Clint's gun cleared its holster. It roared a second time so swiftly, the second report blended into the roar of the first shot.

Sam finally got his own gun out and leveled, trying desperately to sort out all the signals and information assaulting his senses.

Time stood still. Four men stood motionless, facing each other. Each man held a gun in his hand. Smoke trailed lazily from only one gun barrel.

One right behind the other, the guns slipped from the fingers of the man called 'Clint,' then from Lance Russell's hand. As if in slow motion, both men collapsed forward, falling on the guns they had already dropped into the dirt.

Sam turned to face the homesteader at his left. Sorenson calmly thumbed the spent cartridges from his gun and replaced it in his holster. 'You've lost a lot of blood,' he observed. 'We need to get that arm wrapped up some.'

Sam frowned at the man, trying to make sense of what he had seen and heard. 'Who are you?' he asked finally.

'It don't matter,' Sorenson replied. 'The name's Lafe Sorenson. That's all.'

'He called you Frank.'

Sorenson looked at Sam a long moment. Finally he said, 'Sam, sometimes a man learns things he really hadn't oughta know. Things a friend would sure appreciate him forgettin'. We rode in here today, and even though you had a hole in your arm, you outgunned Russell and his gunman, while I was tryin' to get my gun outa the holster. That's how I saw what happened today. I'm askin' you as a friend, to let it stand like that.'

Sam struggled through the haze of his blood loss, fatigue and pain, to make sense of the man's assertion. It finally sunk in. Sometimes a man needed to know his past wouldn't catch up with him and prevent him from building a new life. He understood what was being asked of him.

He took a deep breath. 'I wouldn't want to brag none,' he said, 'so I'd appreciate it if you didn't mention how slick with blood my hand was when I had to outdraw them two fellas while some sodbuster was tryin' to haul his gun out.'

Sorenson almost sagged as the tension left his sparse frame. He recognized full well the sanctity of the unspoken promise Sam had just given. 'I'll try not to blow it up big enough to embarrass you too much,' he said. 'Now let's get that arm tended to.'

21

It was going to be a long ride back to the Indian Nation without his friend Oz at his side. Already Sam missed him more than he wanted to admit. A dozen times a day he turned to say something to the man that would never ride at his side again. Every time, the knowledge he could never share a thought with him again hit him with a new wave of grief.

His arm was a long way from well, but it was well enough for him to leave. Kate and the other ranchers in the valley were past their need for his presence. The secret of Sorenson's past was safe with him. Russell was gone. Grede's wings were clipped sufficiently to be circumspect in his ambitions. Winter was fast approaching.

Eva Spalding had made no effort to hide her tears as she said goodbye. She had tried with every wile and ruse she knew to get Sam and Kate back together. The stubbornness of both of them had proved more than a match for her.

Even Bart Spalding had walked away, suspiciously swiping a hand across the corners of his eyes, rather than watch Sam ride out.

The road back to the Indian Nation didn't require Sam to ride past Kate's place. He hadn't even realized he was riding that way. Now he sat on the knoll, looking down on the yard, wondering how and why he had ended up here.

As if under the control of something beyond his own will, he rode slowly down the hill into the yard. From the corral, Billy's horse whinnied a welcome that Sam's horse answered at once.

Almost at once Kate appeared in the door of her house, rifle in hand. It took her several seconds to recognize Sam as he approached. He was nearly into the yard when she did so. When it dawned on her that it was Sam, she uttered an incomprehensible squawk. She dropped her rifle on the ground, hefted the sides of her skirt, and began running toward him.

As she approached, he stepped from the saddle. Two steps in front of his horse, she lunged wordlessly into his arms. As his arms wrapped around her, she wrapped her own around him, hugging him with enough force that he marveled at her strength.

They stood there that way, silently. She buried her face against his shirt. He buried his face in her hair, smelling once more the fragrance of the soft soap he had cherished so carefully until it was completely gone.

After a long moment, each relaxed the grip with which they had held each other. She took half a step back and looked up into his face, keeping her hands on his sides. Tears coursed down her cheeks. In scarcely more than a whisper, she said, 'You came back.'

Fighting back his own tears, his voice was husky. 'I was just headin' out, goin' back to the Indian Nation. I didn't really intend to come here. I just couldn't help myself. I couldn't stay away any longer.'

'I'm sorry I said all those awful things to you.'

'I'm sorry I paid attention to 'em.'

'I didn't want to admit how much I needed you. How much I wanted you. How terrified I was that you'd just ride away, out of our lives, the way you rode in. I didn't want to admit that I was too weak to even think about having to live without you. So I said the exact opposite of everything I wanted to say. I know it must have hurt you.'

'It hurt some,' he understated.

'How is your arm? It's going to be OK, isn't it? I've been so scared, and you wouldn't even stop by to let me know what was going on. Are you OK?'

'Mostly I've been some lonesome.'

'Me too. Oh, Sam, I can't believe how empty the house has been since you left. Please tell me you won't ever leave again.'

He looked into her eyes, wanting that moment, and the sound of her words, to echo in his mind for the rest of his life. 'You couldn't drive me away again,' he asserted softly.

That was all she was waiting for. She came against him, her head tilted back. He was painfully aware of how long it had been since he'd had a good bath and shave. She was aware only that the man she loved had come back to her.

'Sam!' The excited voice of young Billy shattered the magic of the moment.

Sam and Kate stepped slightly away from each other, turning to face the hurtling dynamo that erupted from the door of the house. 'Sam! You did come back! You're back, Sam!'

He leaped into Sam's arms, throwing his arms around him, burying his face in Sam's shoulder, not even noticing the grimace of pain as he squeezed Sam's injured arm. 'I knew you'd come back, Sam! I just knew it. I been prayin' every night, and I been tryin' to take care o' stuff, and Ma's been bawlin' most o' the time since you left an' I was startin' to think that you wasn't never gonna come back. But I knew you would. I really did. You ain't never gonna leave again, are you Sam? Are you?'

Sam set the boy back on his feet. His arm slid easily around Kate's waist. He grinned as he tousled Billy's bushy hair. 'No, Billy. I ain't gonna leave again.'

Billy grinned from ear to ear. 'You gonna be my pa, Sam?'

Sam's eyes darted to Kate's, seeking and finding the answer he sought. Looking into her eyes instead of at the boy, he answered, 'If she'll have me, son.'

Kate's eyes abruptly took on a mischievous twinkle. 'Was that supposed to pass for a proposal, Sam Heller?'

Sam felt suddenly at a loss for words, and found himself stammering. 'Well, I, uh, that is, I thought from what you said, I mean, that is, well, what I meant . . . '

Kate giggled delightfully. 'Stop stammering, sweetheart. I just asked a simple question. Are you asking me to marry you?'

He took a deep breath, scarcely hearing anything except that she had called him, 'sweetheart'.

'Uh, well, yeah. Yeah, I am,' he said, feeling that it sounded ridiculously lame.

She giggled again. She moved against him, wrapping her arms around him and kissing him. 'Then the answer is 'Yes. Yes. A thousand times yes, Sam Heller'.'

As she kissed him again, she felt him sway unsteadily on his feet. She stepped back in obvious alarm. 'Are you all right, Sam?'

He took a deep breath. 'Just a tad bit on the woozy side. I lost a bit of blood. To tell the truth, I ain't slept too good, neither. I couldn't stop thinkin' about you long enough.'

'Oh, Sam! Oh dear! And here I am talking your leg off! Billy, take care of Sam's horse. Sam, come on in and we'll eat some supper. Then I'll heat some water and let you take a bath.'

He did. They did. She did. Sam's hair was still wet when she made him lie down on her bed. He was lost in the sleep of total exhaustion before his hair had more than scarcely dampened the pillow.

It wasn't anything like she had fantasized it would be if and when he returned. But he was back, and that was enough. When Billy had climbed into the loft to his own bed, she lay down beside the unconscious answer to her prayers and fell asleep, her arm draped possessively across him.

We do hope that you have enjoyed reading this large print book.

Did you know that all of our titles are available for purchase?

We publish a wide range of high quality large print books including:
Romances, Mysteries, Classics
General Fiction
Non Fiction and Westerns

Special interest titles available in large print are:
The Little Oxford Dictionary
Music Book, Song Book
Hymn Book, Service Book

Also available from us courtesy of Oxford University Press:
Young Readers' Dictionary
(large print edition)
Young Readers' Thesaurus
(large print edition)

For further information or a free brochure, please contact us at:
Ulverscroft Large Print Books Ltd.,
The Green, Bradgate Road, Anstey,
Leicester, LE7 7FU, England.
Tel: (00 44) 0116 236 4325
Fax: (00 44) 0116 234 0205